T0148531

# The
# COUGAR
# CHASER

## Cornell Richards

iUniverse LLC
Bloomington

# THE COUGAR CHASER

Copyright © 2011, 2014 Cornell Richards.

All rights reserved. No part of this book may be used or reproduced by any means, graphic, electronic, or mechanical, including photocopying, recording, taping or by any information storage retrieval system without the written permission of the publisher except in the case of brief quotations embodied in critical articles and reviews.

This is a work of fiction. All of the characters, names, incidents, organizations, and dialogue in this novel are either the products of the author's imagination or are used fictitiously.

iUniverse books may be ordered through booksellers or by contacting:

iUniverse
1663 Liberty Drive
Bloomington, IN 47403
www.iuniverse.com
1-800-Authors (1-800-288-4677)

Because of the dynamic nature of the Internet, any web addresses or links contained in this book may have changed since publication and may no longer be valid. The views expressed in this work are solely those of the author and do not necessarily reflect the views of the publisher, and the publisher hereby disclaims any responsibility for them.

Any people depicted in stock imagery provided by Thinkstock are models, and such images are being used for illustrative purposes only. Certain stock imagery © Thinkstock.

ISBN: 978-1-4917-3068-3 (sc)
ISBN: 978-1-4917-3070-6 (hc)
ISBN: 978-1-4917-3069-0 (e)

Printed in the United States of America.

iUniverse rev. date: 04/11/2014

# Acknowledgments

First and foremost I would like to acknowledge God for granting me the incalculable, undeserving blessings and providing me with the opportunity to complete this project. Of course I could not obtain such a feat without, Beverly Anderson giving me birth, and who has been mother of the year for the past three decades. Mom your strength has been simply God like during adversity, thank you Queen for not giving up on me. My Stepfather, Altamonte Anderson who made the best choice in his life for marrying her. It worked out for you with twenty years of marriage. My little sister, Trishawna, who will be a huge contribution in making this a better world, stay strong and beautiful young Queen, I'm watching you. My beautiful daughter Amirah, Your father loves you and I'm not going anywhere. The Browns family, Tara keep up the great work in school, everyone's counting on you. I would like to thank, Tyra White, who worked tirelessly on establishing great communication for readers, and who has also been an excellent friend to me when it was very much undeserving, but was there when it counted the most. No dictionary can provide me with the words that express my appreciation.

I would like to thank, my Self-Publishing Company, Iuniverse for making this recent dream a reality. Dr. David Thomas, I sincerely appreciate your kind letters, and contribution during my brief and trying time. They were just too inspirational and I just had to share them with others. I would like to thank Francis Warren for having a dream about the success of this book and the first to confirm set backs are good. The picture is clearer. Thank you Mr. Abdul Kedar for your good blessings and encouragement. Tone "The PC Man" for recovering my entire document when it was lost and Tiffany Courtney for helping me with the PDF files. I would like to express appreciation and gratitude towards my Community College of Philadelphia Professors. I hope you don't recall me being a headache. Thank you Professor Coppa for being the first to write me a letter of recommendation, it was very special to me during my time of hardship. I would like to acknowledge Dr. Hickman, Professor Jones, Professor Barber, Professor Watkins, Professor Aram, Professors Quinn and Freeman, Professor Ron, and Dr. Pascal Scoles for a job well done with the students in the Behavior Health/ Human Services program. Mrs. Juliet Johnson, I truly appreciate our discussions and your support. Kind regards to my Delaware County Community College Professors. Professor Mcfadden, Dr. Dwyer, and Professor Myers for working with me after a significant absents. Thank you Ms. Donna Ladd for exceptional work, you are employee of the year.

# Introduction

For centuries it has been common for an older man to marry a younger woman without criticism. Ironically society has contradicted its view of individuals from different generations that indulge themselves with what many refer to as a gauche romance. Both scenarios have similar assumptions. If an older man marries a younger woman, he must be rich with the young lady enjoying the wonderful pleasures of wealth. While if an older woman marries, or is dating a younger man, more than likely she is financially stable, maybe divorced and the young stud is also benefiting from her finances. Technology has provided advanced opportunities, which promotes both generations to correspond. There are multiple dating websites that allow you to select your significant other but CougarLife.com is a website that has been specifically created for older women and younger men to converse. You may be fond of the well-known films *"How Stella got her Groove Back"* starring Angela Bassett and Taye Diggs, *"Flirting with Forty"* starring Heather Locklear, and the television show, *"Cougar Town"* starring Courtney Cox.

All three shows are great, but they share the same glitch. These films were all from a female's point of view about the pleasures and complications of dating a younger man. Women love to know the thoughts of experienced and intelligent men. This story is from a male's perspective about dating older women. It's an educational master piece that reminds those who are skeptical of the unusual correlation that not only a tremendous amount of stamina, but love, compassion along with maturity can be found in the youthful age bracket. The concept of equal opportunity should not only apply to the workforce. Although young men are given the opportunity each day to prove themselves in the corporate world. Some may ask why these bios acts can't be eliminated when it comes to dating and being intimate? Allow me to remind you that when Barack Obama first ran for President, many people were skeptical to vote for him because he was young and lacked experience. So if you agree that he's been doing a pretty decent job, why can't a younger man be granted the opportunity to fulfill a woman's needs?

Independence and financial stability is pivotal, and could also be featured on the young man's resume. It would behoove you to select one of these renaissance men, because you would now have the best of both worlds of an inexperienced president who ensures job stability, great healthcare and a companion with marriage potential, providing an extraordinary amount of pleasure. Not convinced? You may recall that Jesus was thirty three years old when he was crucified. Before then he had many followers, he proved himself by demonstrating miracles. After giving sight to the blind and raising the dead, it's safe to assume that he had women constantly lusting for him. So if you believe that Jesus is the son of God? Why couldn't he create a younger man especially for you? Perhaps you would make an exception once the young man has proven himself to be submitable. Still not convinced, well read the story!

# Chapter 1
# Evolve

*Instant Connection*

It was the greatest feeling being the youngest out of the crowd. Being bullied during your adolescent years would be typical, but it was the complete opposite for Carmelo Johnson. He was admired by not only his peers, but some of the older folks throughout his neighborhood of West Philadelphia were quite fond of him. Carmelo was a handsome fella; he stood about 5'9 and 160 pounds. He was dark brown with wavy hair, and for all the years that I've known him, it was only now in his mid-twenties that I could softly hear his Jamaican accent beneath his usage of sophisticated English. As Carmelo resides in the prime of his life, it was not always the case of him being physically attractive. In high school he suffered from a traumatizing case of acme, which was obviously critical to him socializing with the more advanced group of teenage girls. The skin disease sabotaged his quest for making a name for himself as a ladies' man. Whenever I teased him about his pizza face he would vainly reply, "Theo my friend," short for Theodore Smith, "You'll always be second place." Even though I knew that he was only kidding, it was some truth to what he was saying. Even now when we attend guy's night out with our Caucasian friends from Junior College, Sean and Eden, we playfully accept our roles as the smart ones, while anointing Carmelo as the good looking dominant ring leader of our pack. It's not to say that Carmelo isn't smart and certainly doesn't mean that we're not good looking, it's just that over the years of hanging out, we've grown accustomed to his exquisite charm with the ladies.

He and I were about five years younger than the rest of our friends growing up on Dewey Street. He was like a little brother to everyone around him and Carmelo would seldom play with children his own age as they failed to keep his interest; he'd rather not entertain their age appropriate behavior. Carmelo and I enjoyed the company of the older crowd. As preteens we would put on baseball hats and color our top lips with ink just to attend house parties. That's until we were recognized by some of the girls and thrown out by their parents. Learn behavior was the process that he and I perfected and then implemented consistently. You see! Carmelo was being groomed at an early stage of his life to converse with mature individuals; therefore he knew how to conduct himself. He was uncertain about his preference in women, and unconsciously aware that at this point of his life was preparing him to deal with the pleasures of dating an older woman. One of his early lessons were the difference level of respect when dating. All ages of women deserve to be shown respect, but when mingling with the advanced age bracket, respect was more demanded upon making the initial contact.

Perhaps his preference was formed by the enormous amount of affection received as a child when attending church services with his mother and grandparents. However, he would be also taught about disappointment during his early childhood. Jessica Barnett, who was in her early-twenties and the youngest daughter of the pastor, wore stylish hats and was very beautiful. Whenever she arrived fashionably late, Carmelo would be filled with excitement, as he anticipated her hugs and kisses that were more delightful than what seem to be, a never ending sermon. Unfortunately, his fantasy of being with her would never manifest. Before he reached puberty, Jessica married another member of the congregation. She and the bald headed musician still remain in holy matrimony, and whenever they visit from their Florida residence, Carmelo is reminded of the stinging introduction to heartbreak. A decade later those who caught his interest would often mention how mature he was for his young age, but others who were similar to his age, shunned his authoritative demeanor. His conversations of politics and bettering of the environment tend to bore the younger audience, and topped off with his "Mr. Roger's/ Good Times" attire. Eventually experience became his best teacher, and Carmelo became more selective with women, as he was once very promiscuous during his teenage years. His choice of music was also a great quality that easily created an electrifying sensation between him and those he found pleasurable. Whenever we entered his apartment that featured all the trimmings of an eligible bachelor, with no furniture, and a picture of the last supper. His stereo would be glued to his favorite station 105.3fm

You could just imagine how a woman felt when walking into the candle lit pad after an exhausting day and hearing one of her favorite songs from Celine Dion, Mariah Carey, or The Isley Brothers. The pictures of his beautiful daughter Alissa who was five and baby sister Tiara who was seven years old, would surely certify his character, as Carmelo was very family oriented. Although his preference was now to date and perhaps one day marry an older woman, he did not discriminate as he remained open to settling down with someone his age or younger. As the social scene remains to be brutal, he was not always successful in his pursuit of dating women twice his age. Carmelo often said that "being rejected by either age group would intensify his curiosity, while honestly accepting that since the women that he targets are physically attractive and accomplished; they should be well spoken for." He took rejection pretty well, and certainly with class. During a cold stretch, the responses were continuous as some whispered, "You're very handsome, but you're just too young." Fortunately for Carmelo, he remained consistent which led him to finally meet Ms. Larraine Harper. She worked as a Customer Service Representative at Lankenau Hospital in Wynnewood Pa.

When he first met Larraine, it was during our half an hour lunch break. We decided to purchase a few items for the upcoming fall from Old Navy. Carmelo and I worked as Residential Counselors for Don's Youth Detention Center in Springfield. After pulling into the parking lot, I noticed him walking over to a small silver jeep and began to apply his magic. Even though, I did not get a very good look at Larraine, because I was both blinded by the raging sun light and glancing at my watch. I knew that she was very attractive. Carmelo always had high standards whenever pursuing women he intended to be with in public. He was very clever when applying his charm that featured a calm sense of humor. His clean cut baby face, conservative manner immediately had Larraine glowing. He respects the fact that some women are not comfortable exchanging phone numbers, so he simply offers his, which makes them feel more at ease and in power, which so many women may or may not be accustomed to. As I watched carefully for the time remaining on our break, I noticed that he had also received her number, and began making his way into the store. With a few minutes remaining, he rushed and grabbed two earth-color three buttoned sweaters, and paid for my clothes as a kind gesture for ditching me. On the entire way back he kept rambling about how beautiful her eyes were. He didn't even know the exact color, but was certain that they were not contacts.

I took his word for it because he would not have given her so much of his valuable time. There was absolutely no time to waste with a woman that tainted her god given features with fictitious structure. He was very excited to meet Larraine, and even took the chance of scaring her off, by asking her out that same night on a date. Carmelo was a home body, but at times could be an extrovert. "But the first night I asked, good God." He just laughed at me and said that "jealousy was one of the four deadliest sins."

Unfortunately Carmelo didn't get his date with Larraine that night, it turned out that she was babysitting her grandchildren, a two year old baby boy and her granddaughter who was five. Larraine was forty six years old and looked every bit of thirty five. That of course was the assumption I made during the first couple of weeks when she came by our job to visit him. Larraine was fair skin with long brownish hair and had gray eyes. She was gorgeous! Lucky bastard I thought to myself. Since Larraine was a huge fan of Gerard Butler, The classic film, *300* was perfect before having dinner at a local restaurant on their first date. They were dating every other weekend and it seemed that I was left to be his successor for guy's night out. Larraine had never dated anyone that was younger than her, let alone date someone that was young enough to be her child. At age twenty four Carmelo respected that she was a bit apprehensive but was able to keep her at ease. She eventually became very comfortable with him and revealed that she was a recovering alcoholic, and had been clean for eight years. Larraine was also separated from her husband but he remained living with her. The slacker had been refusing to sign the documents in order to finalize the divorce and the details of her failed marriage kept Carmelo doubtful of a serious relationship. So they just classified each other as "Close friends." He was certainly taken by her beauty and a psychological evaluation sure would have been appropriate if he passed up the opportunity to sleep with this woman. "She was absolutely stunning." Things moved rather quickly between the two, and certainly to his liking. He and I planned to meet up with Sean and Eden at one of our favorite places. The Bridge movie theater, which included a great bar and lounge area, with outside seating. We made a pack never to kiss and tell about our wives, and since all three of us were married, it seemed as though we were living out our sexual fantasies through Carmelo.

He enlightened us on how spontaneous Larraine had been every other night in the back seat of his Dodge Intrepid. Carmelo remained living with his parents Mr. and Mrs. Andrews and of course Larraine's home was forbidden. He spent a lot of time working and hoping to return back to school in the near future. Carmelo spent a lot of money during the time he was dating Larraine, money that was intended for him to finally get his own apartment. Larraine often surprised him by sending text messages once he left work and suggested that they meet at a really nice hotel that was not too far from where they first met in Springfield. However it wasn't too long before she gave a blow to his ego by mentioning "Every man must have his own place, and it was now time for him to move out." His parents were certainly not opposed to Larraine's suggestion even though they had never met. I recall her saying that she was uncomfortable about meeting his parents because even though Carmelo was a darling, her children, especially her son were in their thirties and would not approve of their relationship, so she made the assumption that Carmelo's parents feelings would be the same. Carmelo on the other hand, certainly didn't force the issue of his parents meeting his forty six year old lover.

One night he planned to meet up with Larraine after spending all day at the barbershop, which his stylist and childhood friend Tone did an exceptional job. After leaving Carmelo got into an accident which left his car totaled. The Insurance Company failed to cover the damages, so he was now left without a vehicle. Larraine being such a wonderful and generous individual was there to pick him up every night after work. She was even nice enough to give me a ride, to the sixty ninth street train station on numerous occasions, even when Carmelo was off. He now had choices to make, whether to purchase a new car or get an apartment. He decided to take heed and establish his independence. After weeks of searching, he found the perfect two bedroom apartment that still remained in the Overbrook area where he lived. It was a few blocks away from his parent's house and right down the street from his daughter's pre- school. It was also within walking distance from Larraine's home.

Carmelo was pretty good at budgeting, and Larraine was also quite frugal. However since the move was a bit sudden, Carmelo only had a small portion of the deposit to move in, so Larraine extended her generosity by offering to pay the remaining balance. His integrity was what we loved most about him. Carmelo even typed up a written document stating that, he would pay her back in installments, but if he breached the contract, she could take legal action. It was a pretty decent bachelor's pad. The ceiling fans in every room with the newly painted whitewalls created an amazing atmosphere. The freshly cut lawn with bright lamps provided a nice balcony view, which was very romantic during the fall nights. Carmelo constantly filled us in on their exquisite dinners that Larraine slaved over for hours, but was topped off with him providing the dessert. Slow passionate kisses were applied to her neck, as he worked his way down her back, and caressing her toes with his tongue. I remember asking Carmelo during an in depth conversation, was the sex better with older or younger woman? He replied "Honestly, I really don't know." He elaborated that "Although women our age were highly energetic and provided an enormous amount of pleasure, older women that were in their late thirties and forties were in their sexual prime just as we remained in ours, which creates great chemistry. Older women were also a bit more experienced and what's more delightful, was the conversations that were held after what seemed to be endless loving making. "It had been years since Carmelo had a girlfriend and knowing him like many other men, he had a tendency to stray whether a relationship was going smooth or remained in shambles. He began exercising the typical bachelor ritual and befriended a substantial number of women.

Being a young man with independence, he took advantage of every opportunity that was given to him whenever Larraine had gone off to work, or went to spend time with her family. It had been months since they started dating and her husband had still been refusing to sign the divorce papers. This guy obviously had some kind of motive, as Larraine revealed to Carmelo that her husband was experiencing heart problems and was taking a number of medications, which left him unable to perform in the bedroom. One night, during a heated argument after Larraine's affair became obvious, her husband verbalized that some of his neighborhood friends had seen her in restaurants on a number of occasions having dinner with a younger man. Condemned with guilt, she blatantly denied the allegations.

After Larraine notified Carmelo about the confrontation through a text message, he responded by inviting her back to his place to calm her spirit. So she grabbed her coat and stormed out of the house. Inviting Larraine back to his place was a bit uncharacteristic and honestly a very stupid decision that Carmelo was making. What if her husband had followed her? However that's when he and I both realized that he was, or at the very least beginning to fall in love with Larraine. He never would have made such an irrational decision for someone he didn't care for. As Larraine sat on the bed replaying the incident back to Carmelo, he could not help considering that it might be a good time to break things off with her. It was a very confusing time! Carmelo was a very non- confrontational person, but for some odd reason the thought of this dangerous situation also gave them both a thrill of excitement. No matter the circumstance Carmelo always thought of the worst case scenario as he or his family's life could be in danger. Larraine began sobbing and pleaded that it was the first time that she had ever slept with anyone outside her marriage. Carmelo apologized and began consoling her by massaging her back, while his stereo repeated "*Dreams*" by Fleetwood Mack. He made her a cup of lemon tea and gave her two Tylenols for the headache due to all yelling. For the remainder of the night Larraine made herself comfortable on the aero bed that was supposed to be a gift for his house warming party that never took place. She eventually passed out and Carmelo retreated to the balcony and began speculating that this guy could have been one hundred percent healthy and Larraine could have always been an adulterer throughout the entire marriage. About a week had passed and the communication between them had depleted. Although he was well aware of how much pressure Larraine was under in now trying to keep up appearances at home, he seemed to be a bit troubled due to the lack of verbal, more so the physical contact between them. But he never let it affect his job or spending time with his family. In fact this was actually great for Carmelo, as he re- acquainted with us at the sports bars.

It's safe to assume that once in our lives, we all will have an experience, mysteriously transform against us for the absolute worse and now Carmelo would acquire his fair share. Approximately three weeks had passed since they have made love. They had spoken to each other once with Larraine mentioning that she wanted to stop by the upcoming week and pick up her things, which consisted of some lingerie, and a few outfits for work.

# Chapter 2
# Cat-astrophe

*Deception Pending*

It had concluded that they were breaking up with no memo being delivered to either mail box. Nevertheless Carmelo had been working so hard and trying to keep up with all his bills, which were starting to become overwhelming, they never got a chance to meet up so she could retrieve her belongings. It had now been exactly two months without a single phone call from either party. Uncharacteristically, Carmelo remained in a naive state that the reason for Larraine's distance was to keep things cool until the divorce was final. One night after leaving work he decided to sit on his front lawn and enjoy the night air. Sitting there relaxing he saw a small jeep ride by that resembled Larraine's, but strangely she was not driving. She was sitting in the passenger side as another guy was driving the vehicle. Carmelo did not get a good look at him because they rode by very quickly and it was pretty dark. He assumed that it was her son dropping her off, since her husband wasn't known to drive her around. Carmelo wasted no time and decided to give her a call.

Nervously waiting to hear her voice she answered on the third ring. "Hello", Carmelo asked "Didn't you see me sitting outside when you drove by?" "No I didn't, but I can't talk right now." She tried to rush him off the phone, when he asked "So who was that other guy that you were with, your son?" "No" Carmelo became tong-tied and sarcastically asked "So was that your new boyfriend?" She gave a blunt response "Yes, yes he is." Carmelo was shocked, and within seconds of a sure heart attack. He didn't even reply, but his silence spoke loudly. She continued her assault by asking "So when are you going to pay me back the rest of the money that you owe me?" Soon he answered "I've just been tied up with all the bills, but I'll be sure to pay you back, you can stop by this week and pick up the rest of your clothes", "Ok maybe Monday or Tuesday before I head off to work." And they both just hung up. When Carmelo gave me the news, I called Sean and Eden, and we all decided to meet up at a pool hall in center city. Eden blurted, "Could there be any chance that she was joking?" "Absolutely not Carmelo replied, because she would have called back after we hung up. And she tried to rush me off the phone, and asked me for the rest of the money that I owed her, like it was just some business deal between us." I reminded him that "Well technically, it was a little business with pleasure." Carmelo was baffled and furious. Sean chipped in by asking "What type of woman is this, why would she break up with Carmelo and then get a new boyfriend, while still being married? Something isn't right here." I mentioned to Sean that "Maybe the husband signed the divorce papers and then she just met this guy, or at the very worse was already familiar with him even when dating Carmelo".

Carmelo just stood there completely puzzled downing his second beer, as we tried to unravel this woman's whorish behavior. Carmelo began to wonder if her husband did in fact sign the divorce papers, and why she would get a new boyfriend. "Why wouldn't she try to re-kindle things with me?" I asked Carmelo "Could it have been that she knew all along about you sleeping around with other women, but secretly never said a word because it would have made her look like a complete hypocrite to call you a cheater?" He stated the obvious "There's always a possibility, but a slim chance", "But it's still a possible, Eden said."

Then Sean asked what had to be the most profound question of the night. "What if the boyfriend had never existed in the first place and the guy you saw her with was the husband? Think about it, you have never visited her home; you have never officially met any of her friends and children. You only know what she told you." Carmelo pretended not to follow what Sean was saying by mentioning that he in fact did briefly meet her twenty eight year old daughter in the parking lot of our job during a lunch break. He recalls her daughter wearing a brown veil that covered her face because she was of the Islamic faith. "But overall you know nothing of this woman's background. Is Larraine even her real name? We all burst out laughing. But Carmelo remained in disbelief that even though he was intimate with other woman, he was also being deceived and had no clue. It was unbelievable and sound like something from out of the movies. Carmelo had gotten a taste of his own medicine. We ended the night with one last round of pool, and Sean jokingly mentioning "Wow man, she really flipped the script on you." Even though cracking a smile I could sense that Carmelo was hurting. That night I was nominated to be the designated driver. I attempted to bring Carmelo out of his misery and install reality back into his thought process by asking "How could you actually break up with someone that really wasn't yours in the first place?" He just glanced over at me and immediately knew that I was trying to cheer him up by indirectly saying that it was fun while it lasted and certainly not worth feeling down about. "You had a blast, and now it's time to move on. It happens to everyone and now that you have proven that even the best can be misled, look forward to the day that you'll be able to laugh about this situation." I certainly was not happy that this time of despair had fell upon Carmelo, however I did feel a vague sense of being dominant. I guess it was just nice to be the helping hand for once as Carmelo had displayed millions of times during our friendship.

It was certainly not noticeable to others that Carmelo was going through a bad break up, as he quickly began to socialize with a number of college girls and of course the grown and sexy women of our marvelous city. Everything appeared to be getting back to normal until about a couple of weeks later while at work he received a phone call from Larraine asking for the balance of the money that she loaned him. Although he did not have it, this was extremely awkward for Carmelo because he swore never to be in bondage with another woman again. But I told him "At least you can pay this one off." It wasn't only because of the money he still had feelings for Larraine, which was quite normal. She impacted Carmelo; he loved to show her off. Larraine would even make female heads turn and their guys would be offended. Despite being very attractive, the younger women that Carmelo had previously dated could not compete with the Vanessa Williams look alike.

But he wanted answers and felt as though Larraine was obligated to provide them. I have no clue where I was at the time when he received the call, but I think he made the wrong decision by not answering the phone. "Now she thinks that because she has moved on, your jealous and don't want to pay her the rest of the money." "No, I'm going to pay her back the money but I know that's all she wanted to talk about, and she wouldn't answer any of my questions." "So just call her back when you get a chance, do you even know how much you owe her?" "Exactly fourteen-hundred dollars." "Wow, she was really generous, you must have really made an impression." "Of course I did, but I'll call her as soon as we get off work." "Remember Carmelo she wants to keep it as strictly business now, Larraine is not the same person that you met before and she's not obligated to answer any of your questions." "Ok, calm down and take it easy, I'll just let her know that I don't have the money this week, but I'll make it up. I signed up for some overtime next week." Larraine surely kept the conversation as strictly business and unfortunately was not willing to compromise, and even turned up the heat by insulting Carmelo about his irresponsible behavior of socializing and not prioritizing. Larraine wanted absolutely nothing to do with him on any level accept collecting her money, leaving him appalled that she was acting with such barbaric behavior. However her actions defused his temptations of having her back in his life, while urgently anticipating fulfilling his financial obligation. But Larraine made a valid point that Carmelo notoriously became infatuated with the night life.

He had grown accustomed to eating out, at least three times a week and hanging out with us for more than our usual weekend collaborations. It became an instinctively bad habit causing him to be in a predicament. It seemed that he wouldn't be catching a break any time soon. The overtime that he initially signed up for was no longer available. In fact some employee hours were being reduced because of the economic crisis in 2007 -08. Carmelo certainly did not like the fact of owing money, especially to those who tend to behave as a loan shark. I asked him "With all the snuggling up at night and late night conversations, you didn't sense any of this coming?" "No, not one bit, she just began to act extremely cold with no sympathy." A couple more weeks had gone by and Larraine became very irritated after Carmelo once again informed her that he was unable to make a payment. Instead of following the instructions on the contract, that failure to pay could result in legal action. Larraine does the unthinkable, and rather childish. This forty-six year old woman informs her boyfriend about the issue and creates pure havoc by having him contact Carmelo about the remaining balance of the money. Carmelo was never the type to lose his cool but as you could imagine, he was outraged. This hooligan spoke as though he was the one that was owed the money.

Apparently Larraine was very dishonest with this so called new boyfriend of hers. She had given him the impression that Carmelo was just someone in need and he was now trying to take advantage of her, while eliminating details of their untitled relationship. It was obvious that she was manipulating this jerk, while using him to intimidate Carmelo. They spoke briefly on the phone while Carmelo was home trying to sought things out. It was a rendition of a typical junior high school bully trying to take something from a less significant individual. This guy's actions were a complete disgrace. Carmelo's hours at work were diminishing while the harassment increased. As expected, he was completely honest in mentioning that it was more to the story than Larraine had depicted, which infuriated this idiot, who went by the name of Jackson. During one of their conversations, Jackson was boastful about the amount of time that he spent in jail, ten years in a state penitentiary for God knows what. Although a miserable savage, Jackson couldn't help becoming suspicious about Larraine's acts of desperation in having him pester Carmelo. Jackson wanted to know, were they intimate and did Carmelo ever visit her home? Their hostile conversation turned cordial after Jackson persisted in gathering further information about their relationship and Carmelo was willing to expose her. Jackson's curiosity grew intense and remained perplexed about who was telling the truth, but Carmelo answered his questions and spoke with conviction. "Yes she and I have been intimate, and she lives on Tender road, but I've never been to her home. There was no reason for me to visit her; we always hung out at my place.

She informed me that she was married but was going through a divorce." "Yes that's true and that guy is out of the picture", Carmelo comically replied "O, ok congratulations. There's no reason for me to lie about dating a woman especially if I can prove it, by the way some of her garments are still here, and you can come and get them."

The momentum favored Carmelo but he made another bad decision. Why in the world would he invite this lunatic to his apartment? Jackson showed up with Larraine the very next morning as Carmelo prepared himself for work. The doorbell rang; Carmelo looked out the window and saw her jeep parked in the front. At first he thought that she had arrived by herself to settle their differences without any turmoil. But instead soon as he opened the door, Jackson barged in pushing Carmelo out of the way and ran upstairs into his apartment leaving Larraine at the bottom of the steps. Her panties, a few pairs of shoes, work uniforms, and night gowns were packed in a box and sitting in the middle of the living room floor. Although Carmelo was known to be extremely cocky, there was no graphic comparison between the mid age Jackson and the much younger, star studded Carmelo Johnson.

Carmelo was quite taken by the confrontation, and began staring into the pupils of Larraine. Jackson searched through her belongings as Carmelo stood by carefully watching her like a hawk, and keeping a close eye on Jackson for any sudden moves. Jackson began to shout "What the hell is this?" Strangely, Carmelo found this episode to be pretty amusing, as they stood face to face anticipating Larraine's response. Amazingly, she replied that she had no knowledge of the items and that Carmelo had planted them to frame her. It appeared that it was Carmelo's word against hers until he went into his bedroom and returned with a card that she gave him for his twenty forth birthday, which was signed *"Love Larraine"* at the bottom. She remained in denial of having an intimate relationship with Carmelo despite all the evidence that was revealed, which led Jackson to suddenly jump up and slapped her in the face. She stumbled to the floor and very much deserving, Carmelo wished that he was the initiator of the aggressive act. He was totally unprepared, and feared that Jackson would then turn on him. He was actually quite lucky that his daughter or any of his family members were not present at the time of the incident. Carmelo then asked them both to leave, right before Jackson asked for some of the money that he owed Larraine. Carmelo was in no position to debate and pulled out all the money that was in his pocket, which was only one hundred dollars and gave eighty to Larraine.

He then placed twenty dollars on the table to keep for himself. Jackson grabbed Larraine by the throat, while mentioning a few choice words. He then snatched the eighty dollars out of her hand and said that it belonged to him. He then wiped the smile off Carmelo's face by grabbing the twenty dollar bill off the table and placed it in his pocket. They both then left quietly, right before Jackson whispered to Carmelo "Just try to have the rest of the money as soon as possible." Carmelo couldn't help feeling sorry for Larraine. He couldn't imagined how awfully foolish she must have felt, after realizing that although she and him were not in a full-fledged relationship, she was happy. She at least had a partner to share feelings and thoughts with, nevertheless, the great sex. Not to say that Jackson wasn't capable of providing these things, the huge difference was that, she had technically left her husband for an abusive relationship. Jackson informed Carmelo that he repeatedly beat Larraine for her vindictive manner and after being trodden Larraine finally broke down and told him the truth.

You often see in the movies, a hit man being hired to kill someone, buts what's more astonishing is what if the hit man that you hired turned against you? And that's exactly what happened to Larraine. The tables had turned, like they always do when people are being deceitful and malicious. Hard times at work had continued for Carmelo, along with some personal issues with his daughter. He decided that the best the thing to do was, return back home and live with his parents until he was able to re-establish his independence. Unfortunately Larraine never received the balance of the money that was owed to her. She had eventually moved out of the neighborhood, surprisingly it was with Jackson. They were able to reconcile their differences and bought a home together. Carmelo was never the type of guy to go moping around, but in the mix of shaking off the after effects of a traumatizing experience, he would isolate himself during our lunch breaks. During activities with the residents he would seem a little disengaged. But overall I was happy to have my good friend back, who was more like a brother and eventually return back to his old self. Guys night out had never been better, especially now with him being able to laugh about the whole Larraine chapter. It's often said that our experiences are simply just a chapter in our lives and when one is over, another one begins. And about six months later he was fully recovered from the Larraine syndrome. While making his rounds at work, Carmelo mistakenly bumped into Ms. Adriane Carter. He helped her recover all of the pills that resembled a pack of skittles. He first noticed that she had a familiar accent when she took the initiative and apologized for her clumsiness

"O, I'm so sorry she murmured in her soft voice, I didn't see you coming around the corner." But like a charming gentleman, Carmelo quickly took the blame and mentioned that it was his fault. Carmelo felt as though lighter skin women complemented his good looks, rather than someone with a darker complexion. However she was two shades darker than him, with beautiful, long natural hair, and had pearly white teeth. The thing that made Adriane unique was that she didn't remind you of anyone in Hollywood, or on the street and that's what drew her to Carmelo. When they finished gathering all the pills, they introduced themselves, which gave Him the opportunity to offer up a much worthy complement, and ask where she was from and not assuming which could have possibly offended Adriane. She confidently replied that "I'm from Jamaica." "What a coincidence I'm also from Jamaica, St. Ann's Bay." "O, ok I'm from Kingston." "Well it was nice meeting you Mr. Johnson." " O please, call me Carmelo, Mr. Johnson makes me feel like an old math teacher." She gave a smirk and said, "Ok" while mentioning that "Being addressed as Adriane would be fine." "It was nice meeting you again Carmelo, have a great night. "You to, have a great night also." Adriane was an LPN (License Practical Nurse) that worked for a Temp Agency. It was her first night working on the same unit as Carmelo but it wouldn't be her last as they quickly became friends.

Although it was a temporary position that Adriane was filling, she had been doing such a wonderful job that the company offered her a full time position. She declined the offer because our company failed to match her salary requirements but more importantly, she loved to travel back and forth to different worksites and meeting people. The annual Christmas party for employees was coming up in a couple of weeks and Carmelo figured that maybe it would be a great idea if he invited her as a guess. He offered his phone number to Adriane, which he was a bit shocked that she hadn't called him. "I don't know" he said, "She seemed really friendly, but I really couldn't tell if she was interested or not. "This is absolutely one of the worst feelings a guy could have when being attracted to a woman, with her just being friendly and having no interest in you whatsoever. Carmelo and I never could understand those guys who were just friends with these beautiful women, especially if both parties were single.

# Chapter 3
# Captured Cougar

*Rebuilding Stage*

I t was now a week before the party, we're both, hard at work watching movies in the gym with our residents. He decides to go into the bathroom for a quick nap but was disturbed when finally receiving his first phone call from Adriane. He's surprised that she actually called but is annoyed when she mentions that her intentions were to set him up with another one of her colleagues, because she thought that he was too young. Adriane tried her best to vouch for her protégé, but Carmelo quickly displayed how eloquent and determined he was during his pursuit. Overall it was a general conversation that lasted enough time for Carmelo to return on unnoticed of his departure. The interview stage continued the next day as Carmelo and Adriane sat in the break room having lunch and spoke about their work history. Adriane was sure full of plans that day, she always wanted to be a nurse but often considered branching off and owning a daycare center or a Caribbean restaurant. Carmelo had similar interest as he also wanted to own a childcare facility. Adriane stated that she was extremely apprehensive in calling him because he was very young and afraid of what his parents might think. In order to win her over simplicity and his responses would be key, but not to where she would be turned off. Adriane constantly reminded him that she was old enough to be his mother, but he informed her "That's actually great, because my mother encourages me to date older woman. She knows that I am well advanced and should be treated with the best motherly care, along with wifely affection."

Great response, but it was a lie. Carmelo is advanced but Mrs. Andrews would approve of no such correlation. Adriane found Carmelo's logic to be very comforting. Even though it was their first real conversation she seemed to be very cautious in mingling with the young cub, as she was the mother of a nineteen year old. Her son Dane was a freshman at Widener University, and was a Liberal arts major. She informed Carmelo of her true feelings that if her son were to bring home an older woman, perhaps someone her age which was forty four "Under no circumstance would I allow that relationship to transpire. I would give her pure hell." Carmelo pressed the issue, "But I'm not your son and there is a six year age difference between me and Dane, which makes me a valid candidate." Adriane was not married even though she turned down three proposals. A prestigious Artist, a brain surgeon and a well-known politician failed to capture her heart. "It was just not my time yet, I was simply trying to get my life together, and not trying to create one, but eventually that plan didn't work when I met Dane's father." She owned a beautiful four bedroom home in Delaware; her brand new Honda Accord certainly wasn't too shabby as she made it clear that even though she accepted to be friends, it would be kind of awkward working at the same place with her new boy toy.

You couldn't blame her; everyone would surely have access to the freshly developed gossip and spreading your unripe business.

But Carmelo quickly agreed that he was not a fan of being on the jobs front page newspaper. The break room, back of the building, smoking gossiping co-workers would have a field day. Over all he wasn't too crazy about the Christmas party, so Carmelo just decided to ask her out on a regular date and she hesitantly accepted. After all, attending the party together would contradict their purpose of being exclusive. Adriane picked him up around seven o'clock that evening, and realizing that she could have been feeling a little nervous during their night on the town, before choosing a restaurant Carmelo asked her to stop by the super market, where he carefully had picked a dozen blooming pink roses, which earned him a blushing "Thank you, their beautiful" and a kiss on the cheek. This charming mannerism had become extinct during our generation.

They settled for the cozy atmosphere of the Marathon Grill, which was right next door to The Bridge Movie Theater. A bit more confident and relaxed, similar to Larraine, Adriane was doing pretty well for a woman that has never been out on a date with someone twenty years, her junior. On the other hand Carmelo was feeling a little edgy and needed to relax. He ordered an apple martini and chicken strips for an appetizer. They shared bread sticks and after his second drink he couldn't help undressing Adriane with his eyes, as she sported a gray wool mini skirt with a matching sweater and black knee boots. She applied just enough lip gloss, but couldn't help blinding everyone in the restaurant with her smile. It appeared as if she had just walked out of the salon as her hair was fabulous. Although she rarely got a chance to use her gym membership, Adriane was pretty consistent in watching her weight and settled for a chicken salad and Broccoli cheese soup. Her virgin margarita was appropriate for the evening due to the distance in going back to Delaware. Carmelo was able to persuade her to choose a delicious slice of cheeses cake, just so her meal wouldn't seem so deflating. They shared a large bucket of popcorn and a pack of twizzlers. The night was going pretty well, but not that well to where Carmelo would share his beverage, so he purchased two ice teas when she paid a visit to the ladies room. They were seated in the midsection of the theater and enjoyed the action pack thriller *"Hit Man."* Carmelo was a complete gentleman the entire night. On the way back to her car he even opened her door, as she then reached over and opened his.

She immediately turned on the heat swiping away the brisk air from their clothes. After a grand night, the young lad earned himself another kiss on the cheek and too long of a hug, which caused an erection. Her Chanel perfume surely didn't make it easier, but he remained a gentleman. It wasn't that weird as Adriane suspected seeing Carmelo at work. In fact she enjoyed his company, especially when he popped in the nurse's office and held brief conversations, but choosing his words carefully and not tipping off the rest of the nurses that the two were involved. However, when the right opportunity arrived Adriane would have to brace herself from not drowning in his pool of Compliments. I mean, Carmelo would really pour it on pretty thick, and constantly informed her on how beautiful she looks in her scrubs, how great she smelled, and how gorgeous her hair was. But Adriane truly did bring extra spice to the atmosphere with her colorful uniforms each time she came to work. One day I spotted Carmelo from a distance sniffing her hair and telling her how she made him feel intoxicated. This guy was a modern day Casanova!

Strangely it wasn't overwhelming, in fact Adriane open the flood gates and at times would entertain Carmelo's comments with a few of her own, filling his extremely large head. It was quite refreshing and interesting to her that someone so young, and that even worked at her job had caught her attention. Despite her suspicion of why Carmelo was attracted to her oppose to the younger and in some cases more beautiful women from our job. It made her feel good and in her prime that a younger man admired her. She grew fond of Carmelo. His ambition and great personality made up for his lack of independence. She actually encouraged him to stay home as long as possible because he was putting himself through college and having the burden of paying rent would be overwhelming. For the upcoming New Year 2008, I and the rest of the guys planned to stay home with our families, and hoping that Carmelo would have a hell of a story to broadcast once he got the chance.

They both decided to work the second shift which they would be getting off at eleven thirty. The time and a half pay was desperately needed for Carmelo and a little extra sure wouldn't hurt for Adriane. At the end of the shift they both decided to stop by the first church they saw, while giving Carmelo a ride home. A small Baptist church located in Upper Darby, was chosen after she drove by the first three Catholic churches. Time was whining down, as they both rushed in right before catching the aroma from the McDonald's fries next door. A few minutes remained before the clock stroke twelve. The pastor said his final words as Carmelo and I made eye contact. He tried his best to hold in his laughter from us coincidently running into each other. Even though I was unnoticed by Adriane, she probably wondered what the big joke was, as Carmelo continued to be amused. I carefully signaled him two thumbs up, right before the clock struck twelve.

# Chapter 4
# Happy New Year

*Number one Draft pick*

"What a surprise", Carmelo and I exchanged handshakes with a manly embrace." Hey! Adriane, nice to see you." I could see that she had a sense of guilt. She felt busted. She quickly said hello to my wife and two sons and then fought her way through the crowded church, leaving Carmelo to say the good buys. Her abrupt departure would have made it too obvious if it were anyone else from our job that the two were dating. My wife even thought that she was a little weird, until I informed her that Adriane was just caught off guard by our presents. As they both made it back to her car, she began to pester Carmelo with her curiosity. "So that's why you were laughing, did you know that Theo and his family would be there tonight?" "Absolutely not, it was a complete surprise, maybe they were invited by one of his wife's friends because that is not the church that they usually attend." He was telling the truth. Carmelo and I had never made plans to attend the night watch service. "I know that you guys are friends, is he going to mention this to anyone else at work, because that's the last thing that I would need is to be added to your little list?" What list? Carmelo asked, who have you been talking to? Ignoring Adriane's question of Theo possibly spreading the news. "I haven't been talking to anyone, especially not about you." I overheard some of our female colleagues mentioning how much of a ladies' man you are and that you slept with quite a few women in the short time that you have been employed there.

Is it true?" Carmelo's brief silence seemed to confirm her suspicion, but quickly realized that he had nothing to lie or to be ashamed of. He had done nothing wrong, except anticipate lying, just to make her feel better. Of course it was an awkward moment, but nothing close to Judgment Day. He answered rigidly, "Yes, yes it's all true", but how clever of my dear friend Carmelo Johnson to reiterate to Adriane. Is it not all true, what you've heard? Have I not treated you with respect? Am I not romantic and have shown you a great time? So basically you're frustrated because my actions were consistent with what you've heard during gossip hour? Did you ever ask yourself that maybe his reputation is well deserved, since he's quite popular? Adriane gets his point but is still annoyed and answers "No I didn't, Mr. Arrogant." "Don't let a little gossip tarnish our friendship. And hopefully whatever happens between you and we could remain close friends. At least I'm willing to make that lifelong commitment." "Well thank you, and come to think of it Carmelo, that was actually good gossip, but the only thing that I can't confirm was how good that they said you were in bed. "The tension is smoothened as Adriane carefully made her way through traffic. The night sky was filled with an array of colorful lights, whistles blowing and drivers honking their horns. Drunken celebrators hauled their friends across the streets, more than likely in pursuit of the next hotel after party or quiet place to relax.

Surprisingly, neither of them weren't tired after working a dragging eight hour shift. She pulled into the parking lot of a nearby golf club, and continued a very intense conversation of finding true love, while Carmelo was geared towards finishing school, Adriane mentioned becoming a registered nurse was in her near future and would hopefully like to be married. As she continued to speak Carmelo reached for her hand and started caressing her palm. They shared a soft kiss, which seconds later turned into hard and passionate. He's usually very eager, but Carmelo was slightly intimidated by her aggressiveness. She made him appear shy, but he was simply surprised and accustomed to being the one to take charge. Nevertheless, once he warmed up to her, he was back in the driver's seat, until she pumped the brakes and not allowing things to get too carried away. "I'm not having sex with you in my car, that's what I have a house for." "Come on let's make love." "No Carmelo, you got far enough, and not in my car." The scene was surely set, with a full moon shining over the deserted parking lot of the golf course and the windows fogged up. But despite Carmelo being very persistent and ridiculously tempting, Adriane restrained herself and took him home. He'd grown accustomed to rapidly receiving gratification since high school, but didn't want to ruin his chances for another opportunity that would surely present itself and also practiced self-control. She dropped him off, a quick kiss was exchanged and they both waved goodbye.

A nice hot shower would be perfect for ending such a beautiful night and defusing his frustration for not having his needs met. He crept up the stairs to prevent startling his parents and adjusted the stereo from his usual 105.3 station to CD mode. The best of Sade is chosen to maintain his sanity. His H&M shirt is still scented with her Chanel fragrance and he's reminded of their intense delight. However his regular half an hour shower will increase to forty five minutes, and prefers his regular Dial soap scent instead of Adriane's fragrance. His shower is completed and soon as he opens the door, he's trampled by his mother escorting his baby sister into the bathroom. It appears that the little one is within seconds of having an accident, so he makes way before giving them both a kiss on the cheek and wishing them both a Happy New Year. He checks his phone, and there are two missed calls, and a voice mail message.

It's Adriane mentioning that he's probably in the shower, and boasting about how much of a great time she had, and that she would fine out very soon if his reputation was well deserved. Being up and not calling her back would have made him feel too proud, so he decided to bless her with the sound of his voice. "Hey sorry, I just got your message; I was in the shower." "It's ok, I thought you would be, or maybe you just had passed out after opening the door." The shower had calmed his frustration but her voice was reviving his annoyance. However Carmelo remained a gentleman and did not allow eagerness to smear his image. He politely asked, "Did you get home safe?" "Yes, I'm about to relax and take a shower myself." He sarcastically replied "O, that's just great, thanks for that graphic picture." "You're welcome, now you have something positive that will keep your mind occupied, but have a goodnight sweetie, I'll see you at work on Tuesday." "O my goodness I forgot that I still have to see you at work. This just keeps getting better, I'm only kidding! Have a good night." I called Carmelo that Monday (New Year's Day) but I couldn't reach him. He's probably sleeping all day and then preparing for work.

Tuesday morning I basically tackled him, as he sat in the break room having an apple fritter and lemon tea. A quick embrace was shared as he gently whispered "We just relaxed and got to know each", but with a devilish grin on his face. I had a brief feeling of guilt because Sean and Eden were not here. We usually shared Carmelo's escapades during guy's night out, but I surely wasn't going to inform them over the phone, reenacting the behavior of junior high, school girls. We all know that men gossip just as much as women do. Both sex love to discuss what they've heard, seen, or want to know. However there is a slight difference. Women will go to the extreme to inform their friends, while men tend to be more reserved for the right place and time, as I am practicing right now in not calling Sean and Eden. It would not only be cheating Carmelo out of his two millionth headline story, but it can simply wait until this weekend for guy's night out, at one of the local pubs. Of course the guys would only like to hear the ending, and it was not a grand tale being told, but I'm sure Carmelo has a master plan as things were heating up between him and Adriane pretty quickly.

We were interrupted by two of our client's, Casper and Blake along with their counselor Ashley. Within an instant our conversation changed to an upcoming special event held once a year at St. Joseph University on the same day as the Super Bowl. Ashley was known as the ring leader of the gossipers. You couldn't sneeze without her spreading the germs for you. I guess it was in her blood as she studied journalism at Temple University and wanted to be a news reporter. And sure enough in the midst of our conversation she invites herself in by suggesting "Why don't we have a super bowl party here with all the staff and the residents? We still would be getting paid and enjoying the big game?" As much as Carmelo disliked Ashley, he couldn't deny that she actually had a good point. But he stubbornly replied "We'll see how it goes." Casper who was no friendly ghost continued to press Carmelo "O yeah, that would be a great idea, especially if we don't go home that weekend."

Some of the residents usually went home every other weekend and knowing the odds were against him of not working with Casper, Carmelo immediately checked the calendar where it was confirmed that the game would be held on a weekend that the residents would be staying at the facility. Carmelo then attempted to switch days with another colleague but had no luck, and I was also on schedule to work. Carmelo desperately tried to avoid working with this nuisance. The little boy was one of the most notorious and ill-mannered kids in the facility. When his parents got a divorce, his father began abusing alcohol; I couldn't blame him after living with Casper for only a few months. His mother worked the grave yard shift at a toy factory, just to make ends meet. At twelve years old Casper would sneak out of the house late at night and vandalize the neighbor's cars, cut school and get into numerous fights whenever he attended. Constantly disrespecting the other staff members, other than Ashley was his forte. He intentionally lies on the staff and makes phony complaints about staff members abusing him, followed by a frustrating investigation process, leaving the employee in fear of losing their job. Another attempt of Carmelo briefing me up on his sleigh ride with Adriane was not made after they left the room. Speaking of the devil, Adriane enters the room with a smile on her face and Carmelo consumed too much of the tea and burns his tongue.

She approached with a cheerful demeanor "Good morning gentleman" and offers Carmelo a cup of ice water. She mentioned how wonderful it was to meet my wife and children, but felt no need to explain, her odd departure and using Carmelo as a safety net to jump in and save her. She played it cool and made no serious eye contact with Carmelo, as he was doing the complete opposite and basically staring at her tonsils. Adriane appears to be wearing a fragrance similar to my wife's but I'm uncertain of the name. Her sun yellow scrubs brought out her chocolate complexion, which made her extremely gorgeous. "See you later guys" which I catch the quick glance they both give each other as she walks through the double doors into the next room. The day is hectic. Carmelo and I are bombarded with paper work for a dozen new clients and giving their parents a grand tour of the facility. Adriane is not spared, as she now performs a number of assessments for all the new individuals which could carry her into the second shift.

I received a call from Sean letting me know that guys night out would be held at Eden's house for that upcoming Friday night. His wife was taking their children, Marcy and Cory to see their grandparents because they missed them for Christmas. The parents of our new clients admired our workshops and daily food menus, but they were more so impressed with the activities that would cater to their children's special needs. Unfortunately all fifteen new clients were quite distraught and apprehensive about joining our facility although we expressed a normal home based setting and not wanting to make our clients feel institutionalized, as their feelings were totally explicable. The day began to improve, I even think that Carmelo was flirting with one of the single mothers. Adriane managed to handle the sudden case load, as her assessments went pretty smoothly. After work, I informed Carmelo about hanging out at Eden's place, but he seemed to be day dreaming and gave me no response to Eden's luxurious home. "Hey man did you hear me?" "O yeah, that's cool. I'm just a little exhausted." The night would consist of playing pool in his basement, a few beers and Carmelo enticing us with his future thrills for Adriane. While giving him a ride home I could see that he was in dire need of some rest. So after a few hours of sleeping Carmelo was rejuvenated and it was Adriane who offered a night of bliss by calling and rushing him into the shower because she was taking him to dinner.

To others, it may seem minor that Adriane was taking the initiative, but for Carmelo it was a symbolic demonstration of equality that he was looking for, that so many women lacked. Equality was extremely important to Carmelo, as it should be to any person who wants to be treated fairly in a relationship. Oppose to constantly catering to someone and not being treated with the same affection was basically cruel and the general description of a "gold digger." Regardless of their age difference both individuals are expressing good character and obtain a great sense of humor, which are key attributes from Adriane that are displayed during the evening. This is what fulfills the wide gap in years. The two are able to communicate on a sophisticated and comical level. The week goes by in flash; however Carmelo decides to ditch us for his new muse. Adriane's son will be out of town and visiting his father in Tampa, Florida and Carmelo was left to do the honors of comforting her during this brief time of loneliness. We couldn't blame him for switching plans at the last minute, as he seldom did. The guys and I are happy with our lives; we've managed to accomplish the so called American dream which consist of nice cars, a nice house, a beautiful wife, two kids and a dog. It would be on these nights that we would innocently reminisce about our high school and college years of playing the field. We flirted with the curiosity of what it would be like today if we all did not find the love of our lives. Without a doubt, we would more than likely be enjoying every experience at helm. However Sean was never a fan of dating older woman. Eden and I were all for it, as he once had a brief encounter with a Ms. Savannah Jenkins. He had just celebrated his twenty third birthday. She was forty two years old, and was the aerobics instructor for the class in which he met his wife, ironically they also, had the same name. Eden dated Savannah for almost a year until she was offered a new position as a director of a marketing firm in San Francisco.

It was actually to his benefit because he was now less confused and quite taken by the younger Savannah Wilson and two years later out of college she became his wife. I certainly had my share of experiences, one which is quite vivid. Ms. Helen Rhodes, The Librarian that was from Ireland was extremely energetic and resembled every bit of a twenty five year old. I was only twenty at the time, while Helen was forty. I thought we got along pretty well until she decided to rekindle with an old flame that was a couple years older than me. And how could I forget Ms. Zelda Insu, the mixed Philippian and Italian was a forty one year old aspiring clothing designer, who wanted to get married in order to receive her green card. She was heavenly gorgeous, but this ordeal was absolutely too drastic. So she broke up with me and a few months later, Zelda struck gold and married an NFL star quarterback. We're all back at Eden's house as Carmelo calls to apologize again for skipping out on us at the last minute. He's definitely in the mood for romance as I can hear "Trading Places, by Usher" playing in the back ground.

I quickly switched my cell to speaker phone, and all three of us, slightly buzzed playfully begin yelling "Jerk, sellout, man your whipped" and Eden adding a pinching "Be careful this time", which Carmelo ignores but just replies by apologizing again and rescheduling for the following weekend. He wore a black Gap blazer and dark gray pants with black Kenneth Cole shoes. His Polo black cologne upgrades his attire to immaculate and does not conflict with Adriane's Gucci fragrance. He takes a huge gamble and jumps on the bus to purchase some roses from a peddler at the sixty ninth street terminal before she arrives. She had to wait about ten minutes until he returns. She display's her annoyance by mentioning that a woman should never have to wait on a man. But Carmelo charmingly brushes her off and replies "Well excuse me for trying to be consistent." while kissing her on the cheek and revealing the hidden roses from behind his back.

"These are for you", and even though he's in the clear, a very apologetic Carmelo still romantically offers a seductive "I'm sorry for being late". Coincidently she is also wearing all black. Her Armani dress and stiletto heels are exquisite as they dine at one of the fanciest restaurants located in center city. Their immediately seated upon arriving and Adriane is curious to try the jumbo lump crab cakes. A distorted Carmelo is enticed to try the same, so they

order two for an appetizer along with broccoli cheese soup for
Adriane. Surprised at herself of how much and how quickly she
really began to like Carmelo. She informs him that he's fortunate
that she hadn't pulled off and begins rubbing his calf's with her
legs. At twenty five, he was very much a well-rounded guy. Far
more than just having the potential, he was husband material.
Carmelo Johnson knew how to treat a woman. His values and
providing affection sprung from the loving relationship he shared
with his mother. Adriane at no point felt as though she was dating
Carmelo out of desperation. She was gorgeous, intelligent and
constantly approached by successful men that were either married
or wanted to marry her in a short period of time. She was content
and attracted to Carmelo's high level of ambition and maturity.
So after he flips through the menu for the hundredth time, she
thanks him again for the roses and mentions that they came just
in time because the other ones were dying. Carmelo assures her
that he'll make it a high priority so that she has fresh flowers
on a weekly bases, as long as she behaves. Adriane just accepts
his comical rendition of scolding her with a quiet laugh, while
summoning for the waiter who makes his way over after attending
to other guess. Carmelo suggests that she orders first because he
still needs a few seconds. She selects the chicken fettuccini and a
small salad with chardonnay wine. Carmelo disappoints himself
by ordering his favorite as he intended to try something new and
exotic, but settles for the grilled salmon, roasted potatoes along
with a glass of champagne.

# Chapter 5
# Fire Starter

*Benefits Package*

S urprisingly! Adriane is spotted by what appears to be close friends from her neighborhood or maybe nursing school. She had no family members that lived here in Philadelphia and it has been ten years since she lived in Florida and resided in Delaware for the past two years. Carmelo couldn't get a clear view of their faces due to the increasing crowd. However it's Samantha and Rachel, friends from her nursing school. They haven't seen each other since graduation, which was only one year ago prior to this time. Being aware of his popularity Carmelo is already hoping and praying that he doesn't know either of them. Anticipating an awkward introduction, he straightens his blazer and puts on a poker face. As they approach Adriane's smile gets bigger by the second. "Hey stranger", Samantha yells, how are you? They say over each other. "I'm doing great, Samantha and Rachel this is my friend Carmelo, he and I work together at a youth detention center in Springfield." "Hello ladies", while shaking both of their hands.

Rachel who has long brown hair, looks familiar but saves himself the stress of trying to figure out if they have ever met. Carmelo takes a sip of his champagne and is relieved that he has never met either of her friends and remains calm during the switching of their job descriptions and telephone numbers. Samantha a gorgeous blond, with short cut hair, held a very tiresome position at a local hospital, and Rachel worked at a nursing home, which she found to be completing boring except for the salary which was pretty good. The two ladies are politely dismissed by the arrival of the succulent meals, in which the waiter asks "Will you ladies be joining them for dinner?" Rachel gives a polite "No, we just came over to say hello", while Samantha preferable request for her and Rachel to be seated by the bar located in the back of the restaurant. "It was nice meeting you Carmelo", "Likewise ladies." They waved goodbye and told each other to call as soon as possible, so that they could do lunch or maybe have a ladies night out.

"They seemed nice" Carmelo mentions. "I don't really care for either of them, that's why I didn't bother to keep in touch with them after graduation." Adriane didn't like women who gossiped and always in the mixed of things. And that's exactly who Samantha and Rachel were, trouble makers. "They always spoke about everything in class except for the topic, they drove me nuts." A peacemaking Carmelo replies, "Well in their defense, they must have done something right because you guys were in the same graduation class." "O don't be such a smart ass Carmelo Johnson, you know exactly what I mean." "Come on, I'm only kidding, in fact Adriane that's one of the things, that I really like about you, you're non-confrontational. You're reserved and I'm glad that you don't have a lot of friend's especially friend's like those." "Thank you sweetie, you're even cuter when you're being serious. I mean there only a few years younger than me, but you would think that they would have a lot more to talk about minus everyone else's business." Carmelo just smiles at Adriane's little token of wisdom. They're both pleased with dinner, but not as much as Carmelo is looking forward to pleasing her, perhaps the feeling is neutral. He orders another glass of champagne, more than likely to assure his stamina. How disappointing it would be for his nervousness to triumph over his usual thriving performance. Dinner has concluded, the waiter approaches with an offer of desert, which they both deny. Carmelo playfully mummers, "There will be plenty of desert tonight, no need to overdo it", Adriane begins to smile while turning her head; she pretends not to hear Carmelo hinting off the waiter of their passionate moments that awaits during the late night hour. The waiter is amused, as Adriane provides a generous tip with the waiter adding a tad of his own sarcasm "Thank you, and enjoy. "She respectfully end's the dialogue with "I sure will." Samantha and Rachel seem to be having a great time as Carmelo and Adriane leave unnoticed. He playfully suggested that they go over and say goodbye to her friends while entertaining himself with laughter. Adriane urges, "Come on silly, let's make it back to the car before the meter runs out." The night air is cool and when the wind blows through Adriane's hair, it reminds him how sexy she is and finally realizes that's when she looks her best. The ride back to Delaware is a distance, but Carmelo is sure to keep her enthused as he teases her by unbuckling his belt and placing her hand in his pants. He gazes at the lights across the bridge entering Wilmington as she continues the gratifying strokes. Adriane reminds him to call home and "Tell your mother that I'll be kidnapping you for the night." "O yes indeed, how could I not inform my beloved mother of my where abouts, she must be worried to death." His mother answers on the second ring and mentions "I was just about to call you." Carmelo senses a long discussion and quickly informs her that he would be staying out at a friend's house for the night. She then replies with a touching "Ok son, just be careful," and he responds in his adolescent tone "Thanks, I love you mom, have a great night. "The submission to his mother causes Adriane's hormones to sky rocket. Seeing him express his sensitive side with his Queen was a complete turn on.

About three left turns and four right turns later, they pulled into Adriane's drive way. The brick wall home is beautiful. She complains about the lawn and backyard needing to be mowed, and hoping that Carmelo would generously offer a helping hand. Instead still being intoxicated, he responds with laughter and minimally grabs her bags from the back seat as she struggles to find the house keys. The four bedroom house is small, but stylish and modern. Having a hidden talent in decorating, Carmelo suggests that she should eliminate the wall, bringing the kitchen into the living room. Eliminate the huge family table and replace it with a reasonable size table, since she had a very nice eat in kitchen that featured a breakfast table. Therefore she could now enjoy a nice living room without having to go down stairs where her miniature family room was held. She agreed that it definitely sounded like a great idea, especially since she didn't have a huge family, there was no need for the huge dinner table that took up so much space.

She also thought that by removing the second kitchen wall and adding sliding doors for her new deck would increase the value of her new home. "Carmelo make yourself comfortable, and pick out something for us to drink, I'm going to take a shower." The words of him asking to join her almost rolled of his tongue, until he was distracted by the replaying of the ten o'clock news. He made himself a double shot of tequila and chooses a glass of peach Arbor Mist for her. He then decides to give himself a full tour of the house. The guess room was spotless, while the middle room seemed to be used as an extra closet with clothes everywhere. The down stairs den appeared to be her son's mini gym, as well as a dungeon for a mad scientist. There was a number of microscopes and science equipment lying around; so it was safe to assume that Dane may have been some type of lab rat. It was later confirmed by Adriane that he was just studying Chemistry for the semester at Weidner. Carmelo ends the tour just in time as Adriane returns from her shower. He stares at her from the bottom of the steps as she takes a sip from her glass. "Arbor Mist, good choice." Her chocolate thigh peaks out from beneath her pink robe. Filled with adrenaline, Carmelo places his drink on the floor and meets her at the top of the steps and embraces her hour glass frame. He begins to kiss her neck softly, and then the two share a warm long kiss in the hallway before making their way to her bedroom. It's quite chilly, and she apologizes for not leaving the heat on, but Carmelo assures her that "It's not a problem; things will heat up in a minute." It's actually seconds, as her robe falls to the floor and she is wearing absolutely nothing.

Her queen size bed is extremely comfortable. Carmelo exercises the use of protection, while she lowers the volume on the stereo. Their blessed to have the late great Tina Marie serenade them, as they indulge in the heat of passion. Carmelo penetrates, while Adriane grasps on to him for relief of the painful, but pleasurable endearment. Upon reaching a level of comfort, she moans intensely while pulling Carmelo towards her. The first round is satisfying, but more sex than love making. After catching her breath, she slips on her robe and attempts to refill Carmelo's glass along with his order of two slices of potato bread and cheese. The room now felt well over one hundred degrees, so he cracked open the window to let in some fresh air. She then returns with leftover chicken wings, rice and vegetables along with his original order. She's also carrying a filled glass of wine in her mouth. "Wow, all this for me?" "I'm sure you'll work up an appetite before the night is over." Carmelo agrees by inhaling the entire meal later that night. What a coincidence as Adriane turns on the television and the movie "How Stella got her groove back" is playing. After making a trip to the bathroom, Carmelo washes himself thoroughly. Taye Diggs is enticing but Carmelo is superb. Adriane hits the switch and climbs on top of him. She begins kissing him on his full lips and working her way down. Her small mouth struggles to corral his love, as Carmelo rottenly blabbered about being well-endowed. Even though I didn't care for his explicit descriptions, his comments were accurate when I overheard statements from his lady friend's mentioning his performance. Adriane has a young sense of exoticness as she maneuvers her body and the two are pleasing each other in the eminent sixty nine position. He then enters her from behind and their pleasures remained intense and passionate. Round three and four are repetitive.

Before this moment Adriane had never experienced such intensity, not even with Dane's father. It seems to be always forgotten that once two lovers become intimate, the man is not only inserting pleasure but is establishing an emotional attachment. So after Adriane takes a shower early the next morning, she quietly walks back into the room where Carmelo is lying face down and totally unaware that in seconds it will be dooms day for him, as he will be attacked with a question regarding obligation. She finishes up on drying her hair and then sits on the side of the bed, she then nudges Carmelo. "Good morning young man, so are we a couple now?" He pretends he doesn't comprehend and rolls over. Confused and a bit annoyed that she woke him up early in the morning, as Carmelo was known to have the tendency of a vampire whenever the sun struck. She is spared his wrath by the ringing of the telephone, which infuriates Carmelo even more. His grunts sends her sprinting off into the living room. He finds it difficult to return back to his beauty sleep because he can still hear her conversation. Its Dane calling just to check in and to let his mother know how much he misses her. Carmelo quickly realizes that he would still be compelled to answer her question once she returned. So he hurries into the shower and seconds later, she opens the door and hands him a new bath towel and wash cloth.

"What kind of soap would you like?", "Do you have dial, that's the only kind that I can use?" "Well you should have brought some." The door cracks open with Adriane handing him a fresh bar of dial soap, "Thanks gorgeous." Carmelo really likes Adriane, but does not want to rush their relationship. He's surprised at himself for not seeing any other women at this point, but forgot about the speedy affection that women tend to have on him. Nevertheless he holds her feelings in high regard, while being fully awakened by the hot water reviving his body. Carmelo is more concerned about her being hurt and uncomfortable even if she decides to remain seeing him with no commitment. Her sudden question of wanting to be in a relationship surely made him wash his hair one more time before ending his shower. He was sure to hold his ground and was not going to be forced into onus. When updating me, I mentioned to him that "At least a lot of time would be spared, and the possible hate and resentment would be eliminated for his honesty, if both parties decided to just make a clean break." But overall, what if she was only joking and Carmelo was just over reacting?

His thoughts are interrupted by a knock at the door and Adriane informs him that breakfast is on the table. Still uncertain on how to respond, he deliberately walks pass the tall glass of orange juice, turkey beacon and home fries and grabs her from behind. "Good morning beautiful, you look great." "So do you." She softly replies. They sat down to have breakfast and Carmelo prepares to choose his words carefully as she is holding a scorching hot cup of coffee, alongside her cinnamon beagle. "Adriane it 'hasn't been that long since my last relationship but I really like you. It's only been a couple of months but of course it feels much longer because we've established such a wonderful friendship. I told myself that the next time that I get into a relationship I would like to be financially stabled and of course establish my independence, which I so desperately miss." "I know, that's what I adore about you, your dignity. How lucky I am to have someone so young, with so much poise and that is incredibly good looking? I guess, I just got caught up in the moment." Carmelo vainly replies that she has every reason to feel the way she does and he understands why she wanted a committed relationship from him. She begins to ramble, but Carmelo prevents her from beating up on herself by letting her know that he would still like for them to date.

Adriane was actually relieved because she was in fear of being jilted by Carmelo. For the next couple of days he was back and forth from his parents to Adriane's home. She and Carmelo we're hitting the movie theater every other weekend and ripping up every restaurant located in the city. She still hadn't met his parents and Carmelo had never met her son and there was certainly no pressure applied by either of them. However there was once an embarrassing episode that they managed to weave their way through. One day Dane arrived in early from visiting his father. Carmelo was in deep sleep when Adriane dragged him out of bed nude and rushed him into the basement. She attached an emergency lock on the door when noticing Dane's car pulling into the drive way. Adriane was not ashamed of Carmelo, but that would have been a horrible introduction. She noticed that his father was with him, apparently something was going wrong with Dane's car and he came along for the ride, just in case of an emergency.

She could hear Dane getting frustrated after reusing his key and numerous knocks. She made sure that Carmelo was out of site and finally removed the lock on the door. Her excuse was that she wanted to see if it worked, while greeting both men with hugs. When the voices got too close for comfort, Carmelo went out the back door, where he startled the neighbor's dog. Adriane exercise her nature of lying, and requested for them to go to the store and purchase a bottle of corn oil and lamb chops, which would surely buy her enough time to have Carmelo dressed and out of the house. Carmelo's having a ball, her actions were hysterical and he asked "Why couldn't you just tell them that I was the Plummer?" She buckled his jeans and then made sure he had everything, especially his cell phone before taking off like Bonnie and Clyde. They were happy and content, and supported each other. Long phone conversations would rarely occur as Adriane would often drive down to our school and pick him up just to cruise around the city. Although he never got a chance to tend to the lawn, Carmelo would assist with her errands that conflicted with her work schedule. He would often have the car fully detailed, just so that she could spend countless hours at the hair dresser in Upper Darby. Carmelo would now make himself a usual customer for the flower peddler at the sixty ninth street terminal. Not forgetting about his mother, he also made sure that there were a fresh batch of roses on the living room table once he received his paycheck.

After waiting for Adriane to finish pampering herself, he would then treat her to a romantic dinner and they became regular movie goers. Adriane seemed to be always glowing whenever I saw her at work. But she would often isolate herself in the nurse's office during lunch time, while the other girls remained eager to recruit her into their wolf pack. They tried so desperately with subliminal comments and asking her personal questions pertaining to her love life, and how old they thought she might be. Adriane enjoyed having Carmelo as a secret and his feelings were growing for her although he was unsure. "So let me get this straight you want to be in a committed relationship with me, but you don't want anyone to know." But she specifically didn't want anyone from our job to know about their relationship. It could be bad for business. A plague is emerging. Upon arriving to work at seven am, Carmelo checks his mailbox where he receives a memo explaining possible layoffs. He then expresses his emotions when the thought of him getting his new apartment is now in jeopardy. "Perfect timing, guess I'll have to put that idea on hold and walk through one of the three doors that God will provide for me if I get the ax." The newly renovated apartment which was located in Broomall was beautiful and secluded and was close to our job. He's assigned to work with Casper as he sickeningly anticipated on the day of the Super Bowl. Casper was restricted from participating in the special events that would be held at St. Josephs' University. The events would consist of the students interacting with the residents playing board games, face painting, sporting activities with an enormous amount of food that he was prohibited from having. The food was the main concern followed by a huge possibility of physical altercations and stealing items from others once he was denied.

Providing him with room service would be the alternative, in order to prevent any incidents from occurring. All of the residents have completed their breakfast as their departure is now in progress. Casper becomes irritable and defensive after realizing he has been manipulated into the convenient gesture. He is further annoyed by all the jabber and seeing everyone well dressed. After being told to relax several times, Casper pushes Carmelo out of the way and runs into the cafeteria to grab an extra piece of fruit, apparently to take with him. Carmelo tries to calm him down but is limited to just verbal prompts, which Casper blatantly ignores. Unfortunately we are only allowed to restrain the clients in an extreme matter which they are physically aggressive to themselves or others, which has not yet occurred. As Carmelo managed to chase Casper out of the kitchen area, Matthew Givens a resident and a very slow eater began to tease Casper for not being allowed to go on the trip. *Bad Idea!*

# Chapter 6
# Major Malfunction

*Misconception with a little scrutiny*

Casper then makes a U-turn and strikes Matt with a right hook, knocking off his glasses and sending him to the nurse's station with a furiously bleeding noise. The supervisor who was on duty, James McIntyre and resembled Justin Timberlake with a longer face, just stood there like a deer in the head lights. Adriane who was also on duty that morning manage to stop the bleeding of Matt's noise and confirmed that it was not broken, sent him off with the rest of the residents that waited for him in the company vans. Once Matt returned they all cheered and jumped in the company van and quickly made their way out of the parking lot. Carmelo's day gets even better once Casper returns back to his room that was originally made for hospice patients during their final days. There are usually four residents that share a room, but unfortunately Casper failed to get along with others, so he was rewarded the convenience of having his own room to minimize confrontation.

"What's wrong with you, why would you hit Matthew?" Casper then begins using the most absurd language with a touch of the N- word about two or three times. And of course his favorite counselor Ashley was nowhere to be found, offering her helpful suggestions to defuse his raging temper. How popular she was to tuck tail and run during the development of a crisis, while escaping the wrath of questioning from our incompetent investigation team whose job was to basically make any incident appear to be the staff's fault, and justify the resident's behavior by informing the superiors what the staff could have done better. That really pissed Carmelo off and that's exactly why he or no one really wants to work with Casper the evil ghost. Casper's aggression accelerates as he begins punching the wall and throwing various items from his dresser including the television. Casper then picks up a chair and launches it across the room. Carmelo steps back and calls one of the nurses down the hall, where she pretends not to hear him. Adriane is nowhere in sight, but will soon stop by to check on Casper. Carmelo is not fazed as Casper repeatedly yells, "Get the hell out of my room."

He begins biting himself, which now causes Carmelo to begin moving in for the restraint. Casper then flops to the floor, preventing him for correctly applying the technique that would certainly make matters worse. Realizing that he is actually in no mood to struggle with the despondent adolescent, Carmelo backs off and gives Casper the opportunity to calm down. Eventually, the help arrives right after the action has concluded. McIntyre and Adriane showed up wanting to know how Casper was doing. The sight of his room spoke horrifically. Despite being also disgusted with Casper, James asks "Hey Carmelo have you written an incident report yet?" Carmelo replies with a frustrating "No, I haven't but I will get on it as soon as possible. I think Casper should be checked for injuries, he began biting himself and punching the wall while we were in here." Adriane agrees and informs Carmelo to describe in full detail what happened.

Her suggestion slightly annoys Carmelo due to the fact that this is his third year working with a mental disabled population and is fully aware of the procedure, while she has just a little over six months of experience and only provides medication. After Casper's examination is completed it is recommended by another nurse that he goes to the hospital and get an x-ray for his left hand. Adriane is now taking her lunch break as Carmelo and Casper are driven to the Springfield hospital by another supervisor that was also on duty. As Carmelo and Casper awaits the doctor in the claustrophobic waiting room, there is a young Caucasian woman who Carmelo feels that it would be a sin, if he did not pay her a compliment. They began a general conversation, while Casper is glued to the low volume television screen. Carmelo then informs one of the nurses that he would be going to the bathroom and would be getting a snack. He offers the gorgeous brunette a cold beverage but she declines because the doctor would be calling her into the office very soon.

When he returned, Casper is also being seen by a doctor. Everything is going rather quickly, but it's confirmed that Casper has a fractured wrist which Carmelo's incident report explains the reasons for his injury. Before leaving Carmelo notices that the young lady was still in the doctor's office. His charming gesture is actually bad judgment as he writes down his phone number and attempts to have one of the other nurses pass it on to the deceitful woman. Within one hour of arriving back to the facility with Casper sporting a soft cast, Carmelo is called into the supervisor's office. The Head Investigator Salanda Hatfield who caught Carmelo's interest during his first year, smoked ten cigarettes for breakfast, lunch, and more than likely completed her thirtieth by dinner. She informed him that he would be on temporary suspension and a further investigation would be conducted, and if there was no finding of fault on his behalf he would be re-assigned to his duties and fully compensated for any lost wages. Carmelo was a bit discouraged, but remained confident due to his experience of being in this predicament a few times in the past. The previous and most devastating was, about a year ago Carmelo was giving a handicapped resident a shower and stepped away momentarily to retrieve some more gloves. The door closed behind him, locking the resident inside the room. By the time the supervisor was notified who had spare set of keys, and they got into the room, the resident remained in the locked bathtub with the water up to his neck. Fortunately after the investigation, the result was in Carmelo's favor. There was no specific reason for the door having an automatic lock once being closed and no intent to neglect the resident. However, it could have easily been an accident that cost Carmelo his job, and the company, one hell of an accidental death law suit. God is good!

It usually took a few days for a decision to be made, so he began to contemplate his well needed vacation. Carmelo was asked to clock out around nine pm, and told once again that he would be informed of the outcome as soon as possible. Before leaving he informed Adriane about what happened. She was completely shocked but would surely call to check up on him after her shift was over. She had been asked to work some additional shifts for the upcoming week which allowed Carmelo and me to catch up with Sean an Eden. It was on a Tuesday that we decided to attend the Phillies and Mets game that began at seven o'clock. The Phillies routed them, ten to two, with Eden almost getting lucky and catching the home run ball from Ryan Howard. It was his fiftieth of the year. We ended the night at a local tavern, where Carmelo unleashed how well things between him and Adriane were going.

"We have so much in common and the sex is phenomenal. She is so thoughtful, it just feels different and a lot more than just having feelings for someone." The three of us just looked at each other with disbelief that Carmelo was actually falling in love with this woman. Sean whispered "More than just having feelings, do I here wedding bells?" "No that's just my cell phone ringing" as Adriane is calling to see if he's heard anything yet. Carmelo excuses himself but I can still hear him mentioning that something doesn't feel right and that he hasn't heard anything from the bosses. It's been a week and it usually doesn't take that long. He returns within minutes and switches the subject by processing reality that his job is in jeopardy and it wouldn't hurt to begin looking for a new one, just in case the boss's decision weren't in his favor. Carmelo duly notes the offer from Eden that a few positions at the credit union might be available which he has been employed with for the past few years.

Sean reminds Carmelo of his strategy of receiving employment almost immediately, which is sending out as much resumes as possible and harassing as many companies by leaving a thousand messages. Carmelo is young and ambitious; he would surely land on his feet regardless of the outcome. With a supporting cast of family members and great friends like us he would definitely prosper, and what a wonderful addition to his roster in recruiting Adriane as his number one draft choice. Sean sarcastically mentions,"ok golden boy, it's getting pretty late and some of us still have jobs in the morning." Sean almost forgets and reminds us about the barbeque that he and his wife is having this weekend at their home. After having two long island ice teas I was pretty intoxicated so I let Carmelo take the wheel. He wasn't as drunk as I was even though catching a cab or have my wife pick us up, should have been our only options. While driving home, it struck me like a thunderbolt.

In addition to Eden's suggestion, Carmelo also had another safety net. More than likely he would be opposed to the idea because I knew how much he valued his pride and that my suggestion would certainly be a blow to his ego. But I still reminded him that he was still eligible for Unemployment Compensation. He was honestly quite receptive of the second option, but was extremely concerned how Adriane would view him and how things might change once he was no longer employed. Carmelo could not recall the feeling of not having a job. Besides his numerous positions and working odd jobs, since age sixteen he has always managed to be consistently employed. This trying time certainly required a philosophical approach in order to overcome the economic stressor. "If I was to accept being on unemployment it certainly would open a tremendous amount of free time. Maybe I could take a few extra classes for the upcoming summer." What a perfect way to fill the void and utilize his time of despair. Two weeks had passed and Carmelo was still unaware of his status. Adriane had remained working additional shifts and their quality time had been reduced to half an hour conversations and maybe one day a week of physical contact. He hadn't mentioned anything to his parents about the incident that occurred, but he felt uncomfortable and did not want to provide any information until he knew the final decision. He spent extra time at the school library, which gave them the impression that he was still at work. However something obviously has gone wrong and Carmelo takes the initiative, to put an end to his mystery.

He gives the Assistant Administrator Martha Bowens a call regarding his position. Nervously waiting for her to answer, the receptionist Rita Hill is glad to hear from Carmelo and transfers the call to Ms. Bowens. She answers and immediately request for Carmelo to come in, so they can meet with the supervisors that were on duty the day of the incident. Carmelo catches the vibe in her voice and knows that it will not be good news. "Is it possible for you to inform me of my status right now over the phone?" "Well Carmelo it was actually decided yesterday that based on the information that you provided and the complaint that we received from the hospital that you sexual harassed a female, while in the presents of a resident, that your employment here at Dons be terminated." We all knew that Carmelo loved women, but putting his job in jeopardy for them was certainly not an option. It was simply his flirtatious manner that was blown out of proportion. The young lady even went to the extreme and requested to be escorted to her vehicle by a male nurse, because she didn't feel safe. He applied for unemployment benefits the very next day after mentally processing the aggravating blow of becoming a statistic and now being added to the unemployment rate. If it applies, you may recall the frustrating process of being asked a series of questions regarding the separation of your employment.

Carmelo was no fan of interrogation but started to feel pretty good about having the well needed down time, while still being compensated. The customer service representative then informed him that he would be also mailed a questionnaire and a determination letter, which would confirm the exact amount of benefits that he would be eligible to receive. Carmelo now visions the hard part, but feels more confident breaking the news to Adriane over the phone. He's not sure if she has already heard the outcome so he begins to speak to her in a remorseful tone to gain her sympathy. He eliminates the sexual harassment allegations but remains truthful for the grounds of termination which was "Neglect." She's oblivious to Carmelo being fired. Constantly isolating herself from all the negative gossip worked in Carmelo's favor, as she would have surely ignored the accusations. Adriane has the next couple of days off and they make plans to see each other after she gets off work, which gives Carmelo enough time to get home and pack a bag. But not before stopping by a center city law firm for a free consultation. Carmelo attempted to sue the company but it was confirmed by three different law firms that they could have fired him a long time ago for any reason. The employees are not members of a union or under contract with the company. Apparently like many other companies, Dons was protected by the termination at will policy. The document that Carmelo and many of us sign at the back off the application without actually considering being terminated for no apparent reason. Of course the news of him being fired has already sent shock waves through the facility as well as a celebration from a few of his enemies.

A couple of counselors, and jealous old hags from the house keeping department were never a fan of his popularity and stardom. Especially when Carmelo made a sly remark to the daughter of the supervisor. It was safe to assume that witnessing Carmelo's demise was surely at the top of their bucket list. Having the next couple of days off, Adriane is sure to be on the hunt for a new restaurant to dine and inviting Carmelo over to help blow off some steam. The train is right on time, which gets him to the terminal in fifteen minutes. He waits only a few minutes for the sixty five bus and is home in an half an hour. He's greeted by his sister and stepfather Mr. Andrews. His mother is upstairs taking a nap and the little one is in her usual playful mood. Carmelo pauses his proceedings to briefly entertain the princess. Hugs, kisses and a little rough housing are exchanged by the siblings. Carmelo looks at his watch that was given to him by his mother for his twenty fifth birthday and realizes that he still has plenty of time remaining until Adriane arrives.

The rush hour traffic is sure to add an extra twenty minutes, so a quick spelling test would be perfect. The little genius races through the words and then is called to bed by their mother. Before sending her off, Carmelo slips a ten dollar bill into her pocket and kisses her on the cheek. "Good job baby girl, have a good day in school tomorrow." She then mimics him while running up the steps and then heads into the shower. Mr. Andrews is fast asleep on the couch with the television watching him. It's obviously not the right time to spring the horrible news on his parents, and

Adriane will be arriving shortly. He knocks on his mother's door to say goodnight and tickles the princess before finally getting ready to leave out. Adriane calls to make sure that he will not have her waiting. He hops into the shower and then packs two of everything in his messenger bag. He then heads down stairs and looks out the window just as Adriane finally arrives.

He carefully shuts the door leaving his stepfather on the couch passing gas in his sleep. He jumps in the car, greets Adriane with a sloppy kiss and she speeds down City Avenue. There's no reason to remind him of his consistent excellent dress code, but she is quite taken by his Sean john, King Cologne. "Why you're looking rather dapper for a man that's unemployed. He cleverly answers "All for you young lady, all for you." "Hey Carmelo I would like to go and have dinner somewhere that I haven't been in a long time." He jokingly replies, "Try the kitchen." It was actually a response that he reiterated from one of his favorite gangster films "*Good Fellas.*" "Hey Carmelo you're really not that funny. And how would you like it, if I actually turned that into a reality, for me to rarely make you a home cook meal." "Ok ok, but I'm really not that hungry, let's just grab something quick and head back to your place."

She gives in and settles for Chinese. The two courts of fried rice, egg rolls with Broccoli was actually a good call by Carmelo as her appetite was filled after a small portion. They went back to her place and cracked open a bottle of wine to celebrate the much needed romance. No discussion was held about him losing his job, that's how ambitious my dear friend Carmelo had been. It really didn't matter because he would be just fine, especially with the strong support of his family and great friends like us, to make sure he remains on cruise control. Early the next morning Carmelo is awakened by the clashing of the pots and pans. He's quickly smoothed over by Adriane kissing him on the cheek and rubbing her fingers through his wavy hair. He expects the usual turkey beacon and home fries, but she puts a spin on breakfast by adding strawberries, and cantaloupes. Which are Carmelo's favorite fruits. Her little treat was more than likely to complement the young prince for his performance. He disregards having table manners by chewing loudly and explaining his master plan of simply taking additional classes at our Community College so that he could graduate in the spring, while receiving his Unemployment benefits. "Lucky you, free money and then graduating college, I knew that I didn't have to worry about you. Excellent plan young man, so Car-lazy-o, Are you going to help me clean the house or just sleep all day?" "You think that I would actually just sleep all day and not make love to you. I'm not that lazy" as he got up and began chasing her around the table. "Stop Carmelo, I'm tired." "Ok no problem, relax and get some rest. And by the time you get up, this mini mansion will be spotless." She looks at him with a huge sense of doubt but he convinces her that he can be trusted and she takes a long nap into the guess room. It was the least that he could do after what had transpired, Adriane was clueless and more than likely would remain in that stage.

He begins his house duties and to his benefit the master bedroom is the only room that needs to be cleaned due to their intense activities in the night. Adriane seemed to have a rare case of OCD (Obsessive, Compulsive, Disorder) and kept her home in immaculate form. The lawn and back yard was taken care of by Dane before leaving to spend the night at a friend's house for the weekend. It took exactly five minutes for him to finish cleaning. Adriane was actually more interested in getting some rest rather than tending to a few unfolded sheets and clothes. After downing a health shake, Carmelo just made himself useful by listening to some music on YouTube and checking his email. With absolutely no intensions to become a singer Carmelo just hums to "Krush Krush by Paramore." About two hours later Adriane woke up and followed the annoying sound. She crept up quietly and scared the crap out of him. "What the hell? Hey Adriane I would like to live past your stone." "O please, hush, but thanks for cleaning up." "Anytime beautiful." She sits on his lap and mentions that there's a church service that will be held at seven o'clock. They have a few hours until it's time to head out, so she expresses her gratitude to Carmelo for keeping his promise. It was now Carmelo who was in much need of a nap. Adriane selected a turquoise dress and almond stilettos for the evening sermon. She then Ironed Carmelo's Brown dress shirt and khakis before taking her shower. He remained sleeping down stairs until she begins screaming and rushing him into the shower. Carmelo needed additional time to be rejuvenated, but almost caused them to be late. She loved to be punctual, as he stared in the mirror she packed him a snack that appeared to be for a two year old, and they were out the door. Even though the suggestion of going to church was sudden, it demonstrated how much their relationship had progressed.

# Chapter 7
# Nothing Strange

*Same Page*

Attending the latest movies and going to nice restaurants was the easy part, because their all social areas, but attending religious ceremonies was emblematic and pure. This was an experience that they only shared with their family members and close friends. It was the first time that Carmelo ever went to church with a woman. Their comfort level was splendid and without a doubt, envied by others. They didn't have to put on a show for anyone, they could just be themselves. The church was huge but appeared to have only been in existence for a short time, possibly less than ten years. Judging from all the cars in the parking lot it was safe to assume that the service would have a vast number of worshipers. "Come on Carmelo all of the good seats will be taken. "Strangely, as soon as they opened the double doors there were exactly eight people in attendance. Carmelo fines humor and asks is this place really that boring? Adriane pinches him on the right thigh and then asks the lovely young couple in front of them, "Where is everybody?" The young lady replied that there is a concert featuring a well-known R&B singer and that the church offered parking space for a small fee.

The pastor applauds the few members and visitors that arrived by mentioning "God grants millions of blessings but what a shame, only few are willing to accept his word" Carmelo dozed off and was pinched again an hour later as the service was ending. They departed from the church holding hands and waving goodbye to the ushers who gazed in suspicion. Carmelo just continued to smile and gave Adriane a kiss. It was still early and she suggests that they stop by Wal-Mart and purchase some new under wear for him. She was able to maneuver two accidents, while Carmelo jokes about her having road range. He was attempting to make the transition from boxers to biker briefs and figured that the snug fit under wear would be perfect for his model shaped frame. Apparently a lot more people liked shopping at Wal-Mart on a Sunday night, than going to church, as the parking lot was jammed packed.

Carmelo acknowledges that despite the crowd they should be in and out in no time because the lines were moving pretty quickly. "Three minutes tops", he boasts. "Wow that sounds like sex with you Carmelo." "Really" "O relax you know I couldn't let that one go." "Very funny, and how would you like for me to make that a reality?" "Just go and pick out your new panties pretty boy." He stops by isle number four and is a bit confused on which colors to select. He's careful in not wasting too much time and chooses the medium size black, gray and navy blue three pack. He returns to Adriane who is struggling to carry the hand basket and takes it from her before she continues to strain. "Here grandma let me give you a hand." She then attempts a third pinch, but Carmelo dodged the playful torture. She pays for the items and there out the door. One hour total was spent in the store as Adriane continued the typical routine for women to be undecided and spending an enormous amount of time when shopping.

"It felt like forever." She only purchased some can goods and a few personal items. There back at her place in no time. Carmelo is exhausted after having a long day of sleeping drinking and love making, buts hops in the shower and is now eager to try on his new pair of under wear, while she puts away the groceries. He selects the black pair and walks into the kitchen attempting to seduce her. She compliments him on how great they look as she adjusts the table mats. The chicken fingers with rice and carrots hits the spot as the two just spent the rest of night conversating on how their relationship as grown and whether it would go any further. Adriane is suddenly in the mood for having a movie night but before choosing a flick she prepares a second plate for Carmelo and allows him to decide on the movie. He searches through the channels for a horror flick, which she objects after catching a glimpse of "*Michael Myers H20*". "*Along came Polly*" starring Ben Stiller and Jennifer Aniston is more appropriate for the evening. Neither one of them remembers the forecast mentioning rain; however it begins to thunderstorm. She removes her robe and cozy up next to her stud. Her all black Victoria Secret lingerie is alluring but Carmelo retrains himself momentarily and just enjoys the view under the oversized blankets. The love story has captivated the two fornicators, and they both willfully succumb to each other's desires. But as he reminded me, after the caressing and loving making the most potent was the mental affection.

It continues to rain in the morning as Adriane prepared for work. She will be heading to another site in Ardmore. A school where the students are handicapped and mentally disabled. She takes Carmelo to the nearest bus station and right before they depart he urges her to be careful while driving and extends a good day kiss. Carmelo returns home soaking wet and finds a note on his dresser that his mother has taken his little sister to school and after that she would be running a few errands. He's a bit annoyed because this would be the perfect time to inform her that he had lost his job. The feeling of discouragement begins to kick in that he is no longer employed and has the luxury to lounge around with me and our residents, as he and I often entertained ourselves doing absolutely nothing. Removing his wet clothes and taking a hot shower would certainly make him feel better, while listening to the hilarious *"Steve Harvey"*, morning show. He then took a long nap and woke up around noon. His mother had arrived and Carmelo was looking forward to putting an end to his secrecy. It was only common courtesy to allow her to get settled, but after then he kissed her on the cheek and simply explained that things have been a little rocky at work and that he was fired last week. He continues to mention that he has been hiding out down at the school to occupy his time until he was informed about his status. Like the loving and devoted mother she has always been, Mrs. Andrews simply informs her beloved son that he can remain in her home until he's fifty.

She's only a bit disappointed that he hadn't inform her at first. Placing a financial burden on his parents was certainly not an option so he kept his termination private. He assured his mother that this was more than likely a blessing, because he can now apply more focus toward his education, as he would still be receiving an income through his UC benefits. Adriane began working a tremendous amount of hours, leaving their well engaged relationship temporally detached. This went on for about a couple months and it was obvious that their relationship was taking a toll. One night during an in depth conversation, Adriane mentioned that maybe Carmelo should pursue someone is own age. Unexpectedly she doubted that either of them would be happy and she did not want to hold him back. But Carmelo simply replied that he wants the best for her and hopes that she is not trying to ditch him for someone else, which she instantly denied. She was more concerned about hindering his progress of actually finding his soul mate. He was content with Adriane, and finding his soul mate at the moment was actually the last thing on his mind. Carmelo continued to feel the wrath of a scorn woman and rarely got a chance to spend time with his daughter. Things had entered the gray area between him and Adriane, but whenever the opportunity presented its self she always gave words of encouragement, in fact she even expressed her generosity by assisting Carmelo with his school tuition as graduation was now only a couple months away. A month goes bye and his UC benefits finally kicked in. He immediately made plans to write a check for his mother towards the bills and to pay Adriane back. He has flash backs of how his relationship ended with Larraine as he makes his way to center city, en route for the T-Mobile service giant.

Amazingly his forty dollar a month phone plan is now seventy dollars. Carmelo loved center city. It was a therapeutic destination whenever he needed comfort from stress or wanting to feel important by mingling with individuals of higher significance. While leaving the store he spotted Melanie Rollins who was on her way to have lunch. But before making his approach, Carmelo clutched his newly purchased, self-help book, *"Reposition Yourself"*, by Bishop T.D Jakes. The sight of young black handsome male carrying a self-help book spoke for itself, as Melanie later confirmed that was very appealing. The twenty four year old accountant was gorgeous. Melanie graduated from Millersville University, and worked for a small company in center city. Being in charge of accounts receivable was just an occupation that paid the bills. Similar to Adriane, Melanie was sure full of plans that day as her primary goal was to move to Las Vegas and become a certified financial planner. Carmelo immediately charmed her by offering to pay for lunch as they chose a quiet section in the local gallery and got to know each other. It was a coincidence that they both attended Overbrook High, but never recalled seeing each other. Melanie graduated one year ahead of Carmelo in 2001. They lived within twenty minutes apart, which she resided in the Germantown area of the city. Melanie shared her charming one bedroom apartment with her cousin Robert, who she allegedly kicked out because of Carmelo. Carmelo actually tried to withdraw from their friendship when Robert expressed verbal aggression towards him.

Robert was just intimidated by his presence and was no longer the so called man of the house. Despite the awkwardness, Melanie and Carmelo continued to be friends. In fact she invited him to her neighbor's birthday party, which would set the stage for him to shine amongst the family of females. Carmelo insisted that he purchase a gift, but Melanie thought it wasn't necessary, but finally agreed that a baseball hat would be perfect for her lesbian neighbor. She later confessed that at the time she was struggling financially and feared being outshined by Carmelo when he showed up with a gift for someone he didn't know. Carmelo had never socialized with same sex couples. But Courtney and Paige were cool. Courtney even made frozen drinks with whip cream whenever he visited. That night he rose to the occasion and mesmerized the ladies by explaining his political views during the historical presidential election. Later that evening Carmelo turned up the heat by assisting an elderly woman to the restroom. His mannerism earned him an enormous amount of brownie points because the crippled woman was actually Courtney's mother. Melanie stood in amazement as Carmelo's sensitivity dazzled her entourage. He was offered to spend the night for his stellar performance, and with great pleasure, he accepted. Adriane continued to work as if she was feeding a village and their fragile communication was close to nonexistent.

Melanie and Carmelo got along pretty well. Carmelo had begun spending more time with his daughter and Melanie made the best of it by planning an outing at the Please Touch Museum. They also brought along his little sister and her best friend Tina. Afterwards, they all relaxed at the elegant water fountain that was close to the museum. Weeks later Melanie's niece had a lavish first birthday party that included Elmo, Big Bird, and a clown who was the host of the party. Carmelo did a great job catching all of the action on his phone. It was a complete shocker to me that Elmo could actually pull off doing the break dance. Besides the numerous dates, attending Melanie's baptism was a tremendous experience as she gave her heart to the lord. Shortly after making her great decision to walk in Jesus's footsteps, she would be forced to make another huge decision.

Except this time, it would cause her to take a million steps backwards as it was confirmed by her gynecologist that she was a few weeks pregnant. Her decision to have an abortion couldn't have arrived at a better time. She was barely making her rent on time and paying her car note. Never mind the host of family members and friends that needed to borrow money from her around the same time that all her bills were due. Out of the kindness of his heart Carmelo granted her favors whenever he had the opportunity. Neither of them were in a position to have children, so Melanie bit the bullet and scheduled an appointment to receive counseling before having her procedure. This covert discussion took place just as Carmelo knocked down the eight ball during an intense pool game between him and Eden. We quickly changed the subject and conversed about graduation night. A trip to Atlanta was in progress but first Carmelo wanted to make sure that he was going to be participating in the ceremony. His *Group Dynamics,* professor that he found absolutely repulsive was actually nice enough to provide him with additional time to submit incomplete assignments in order to receive a satisfactory grade.

Her teaching style was so dreadful that Carmelo just disregarded the assignments but eventually put himself in a predicament. He spent the night with Melanie and consoled her as they prepared themselves for her early morning procedure. When he and Melanie approached the parking lot they were greeted by screaming protesters holding pictures of a mutilated fetus. This isn't the first time for either of them as Melanie shared this traumatizing process with her previous boyfriend. We often joked that Carmelo should have been rewarded with V.I.P access, since he seemed to be a visitor every other month. After the eight hour shift of sitting in the waiting room, he drove her home and just relaxed for the rest of the afternoon. The medicine that Melanie was given was still in effect and she remained in dream land, so Carmelo went for a walk and enjoyed the spring air. Apparently Adriane has a few minutes to spare as his phone begins to vibrate with her picture appearing on the screen.

What a treat that would have been for Melanie, if she saw Adriane's picture and answered his phone. Turmoil was the last thing he needed. He answered and expects the usual two minute drill. His anticipation is correct but this time Adriane includes plans for dinner and a box of cigars. A premature celebration as she will be swamped with work for the month of May, which caused her to miss our graduation. He also knew that this would be a perfect opportunity to pay her back the money that she loaned him for his school tuition. They planned to meet at a small Italian restaurant in the city that was well known for politicians and other corrupted law makers. He returned back to Melanie's house with a glass of wine and dinner prepared for him. Melanie made the most delicious hot chicken strips with potato wedges. Even though the microwave did most of the work, they still came out pretty well. After having dinner she remained in bed and he returned home.

Graduation was less than a month away, Carmelo managed to turn in the work before the dead line and it was confirmed through an email that his professor successfully received the assignments and that he would be graduating. After getting the good news he treated himself to a new outfit to have dinner with Adriane. Her white banana republic dress is refined and collaborates well with his black photographer pants as he sported a white tee shirt beneath a light gray blazer. The weather is great and they chose the outside seating area while immediately ordering two pineapple parrot bay drinks on ice. Carmelo doesn't eat red meat but for some reason he has a craving for steak and potatoes along with a side of broccoli. Adriane orders the same with a shot of Jack Daniels indicating to Carmelo that she must have had a rough day, or perhaps a rough few months since it's been a while that they have spent any time together. She jokingly asked, "So who's the lucky girl?"

How typical of Carmelo, who begins to smile ridiculously after being put on the spot. True in deed Melanie was lucky to have Carmelo, but the feeling was not mutual. Despite her accomplishments and physical appearance, Melanie lacked showing affection on many occasions when it was mostly needed. He never felt a rush, which creates chemistry between two lovers. Carmelo was a kissy, Romeo kind of guy which conflicted with Melanie's lackluster display of affection. Furthermore, Carmelo despised women that choose the club scene for their social areas and he stressed that to Melanie over a million times. About a few weeks after her procedure, the genius applies and receives a part time job, working as a party associate at a night club in a high crime, drug infested area. Their relationship deteriorated due to similar issues as Adriane with a commanding work schedule. It made spending time with each other very difficult, which Carmelo did not object, and was happy to have less explaining to do for their demise. The interest was gone on both sides. He made an attempt to resolve their differences by asking her out to dinner, but she declined and expressed no further interest.

It felt as though he had dropped the last piece of apple pie from Tasty cake. But a main course meal would be more fulfilling. And that's why he and Adriane are both here, enjoying the fire that sprouted in the beginning of their relationship. What a crafty little fella, as he informs Adriane that no one is luckier than he is, to have such an opportunity to dine with one of God's most precious creatures. He then slips a massive wad of cash into her palm and says, thank you. A trio of young ladies were seated diagonally from them, overheard Carmelo and began giving Adriane dirty looks. As the cool night air becomes chilly, they both move their seats into the bar area far away from the invidious group. They try out the cigars, which are perfect with a shot of Brandy and indirectly attempting to establish a new tolerance for alcohol as they each took a shot of tequila and hit the road to a nearby hotel.

# Chapter 8
# Congratulations!

*Welcome back to the Liacouras Center*

I t's a great day for me and Carmelo. Broad Street is packed with the support of family and friends for the graduating class of 2008, the Community College of Philadelphia. Carmelo is blessed with the presence of his daughter who is in attendance with his little sister and grandparents. His parents hold back tears while posing for a few pictures. Their all here to witness this milestone in his career. His aunts and cousin are running late as the procrastinators are sure to be adding the finishing touches to their hair and makeup. Adriane texted several times to apologize for missing the graduation. However, Melanie was even nice enough to stop by and take a photo or two with Carmelo. She even purchased him a graduation teddy bear, which he still has somewhere in his walk-in closet. He remained comfortable in the spot light soaking up all the pleasures of this moment. After taking a few pictures with him, I ran over to my professor and asked her to join me in a family photo. She then praises my mother for a job well done in raising a King, but within seconds the intellect is kidnapped by another pupil for photos. My skin was melting under the oversized black gown. All four hundred students were ushered into the basement of The Liacouras Center to be relieved from early morning eighty degree heat.

The graduation Coordinator makes an announcement and directs the students to go to their assigned section, which is according to our course of study, but she's totally ignored by the intense celebration. Carmelo and I are corralled by some of our female classmates. Hugs, kisses, and even happy tears are being shared by those who were skeptical of this great day. It's only Junior College, but for Carmelo and I this day was nonexistent. While growing up, we lived a different, more corrupted life style, but had now proven that the transition was made in order to help others make better decisions in their lives. I saw Carmelo taking extreme interest in a woman, but it was a huge celebration, so it was safe to assume that the conversation was platonic. We finally made our way to the auditorium which was full of pandemonium from the crowd. Our seating arrangements were different but Carmelo managed to sneak his way over to keep us together.

When he sat down beside me with a huge smile on his face, I immediately knew that something had already happened or was surely in process of happening. Before I could ask, "What did you do?" The announcer calls my name and my picture appears on the twin wide screen monitors for the audience seated in the upper levels. The noise is excoriating as my family is buried in the crowd. A few other names are called before Carmelo's with the same result. The President of CCP begins his boring half an hour speech, which he never stopped by the college during the year to offer five seconds of encouragement. But this is a perfect opportunity for Carmelo to inform me of the scam he's trying to pull off. He continues to grin devilishly and whisper "She's so beautiful, I haven't seen her since the beginning of the semester", as he is referring to Ms. Belinda Simmons, who withdrew from their Group Dynamics course that they both attended in the beginning of the term. Just like Larraine and Adriane, Belinda was immediately captivated by Carmelo's persona.

What better place, besides church to meet someone? Belinda was actually quite surprised, because Carmelo had enough time to make his advancements. They sat next to each other a few times and sometimes waited around together whenever their professor was running late for class. He never mentioned this woman at all while dating Adriane and Melanie. Newly elected and extremely late, Mayor Michael Nutter makes his way to the podium and begins his speech. The new alumni's are tired and bored to death. The well-known Philadelphia crowd begins to express their frustration with taunts of booing and rushing him off the stage. Right before the President returns to send us off; Belinda sends her phone number down two rows for Carmelo. Members of the student government committee begin smirking and patting Carmelo on the back. What a classic moment indeed. A final "Congratulations to the class of 2008 is mentioned by the President" with our caps being tossed in the air and everyone made a clean exit.

Broad Street is now twice as packed, due to a second ceremony being conducted for some high school graduates nearby. Last minute photos are taken and Carmelo's daughter is getting annoyed with all the attention that her father is receiving from his female fans. So after spending time with our families, Carmelo and I planned to meet up later that night in old city. More than likely we would be celebrating with the rest of the other graduates from other schools. After several minutes of trying to decide where to have lunch, my family and I settled for The Continental. I remembered Carmelo mentioning that we should go there for guy's night out. They actually had two locations, but eighteenth and walnut was perfect. The restaurant was fabulous and had great service. They offered a delicious brunch menu, as it remained very early in the day. Carmelo sends me a text and mentions that he would be going straight home for a preferred home cook meal and to relax because he was exhausted. He's energized by his cousin, as she dragged him to the Old Country Buffet where he had three meals and a host of elderly folks repeatedly congratulating him. A great deal of rest was needed for the wild party that awaited us at midnight.

As expected it came in a flash. Second and Market Street was jam packed, third and chestnut was going bananas with horns honking and women exposing themselves for what appeared to be their last dance, before entering the corporate world. We chose a nice lounge area with a dance floor. Sean and Eden decided to bring sand to the beach, and sour down the night by inviting their wives. As I mingled around the room, Carmelo made himself a home at the bar and chatting up a few alumni's from a local university where he and I planned to get our bachelors' degree. A strange character emerges from the booths and begins dancing like a mad man, kicking off his shoes and dancing barefooted. He's obviously had too much to drink, but Sean and Eden encourages him to continue his foolish performance. The bouncers rushed over and politely ask the gentleman to put his shoes back on, or leave immediately. The startled women that Carmelo was entertaining were no help as they offered the drunken fellow shots of Hennessey to continue. Shortly after the young ladies began to make an early exit, I joined Carmelo at the bar. He described in graphic detail, the plans that he had for his well anticipated new experience. Earlier he reached a mile stone in his career but now he'd reach another one in his social life in connecting with the fifty year old Belinda Simmons.

This was surely an experience that Carmelo could not wait to grasp. Even though he never used the term cougar, he informed me that women between the ages of fifty to sixty were referred to as Panthers. In fact, Corner Canyon high, a new school set to open in Draper, Utah in 2012 had its request for a team nickname, the Cougars, which was the number one choice in a poll of future students, rejected by the school board on the grounds that it would be offensive to some middle aged women. Carmelo called Belinda about a week later after graduation. It was a rather challenging discussion as Belinda began attacking him about his financial status, which he immediately came clean about receiving unemployment benefits. She was extremely concerned about him being in his mid-twenties and remained living with his parents. Her generation was accustomed to parents kicking their children out of the home at age eighteen, to support themselves. And according to her standards Carmelo was far passed the deadline. It made him very uncomfortable, but the brainy lad kept his composer and acknowledged the fact that even though being turned off by her cut throat demeanor, he would eventually convince her that this would be one of the greatest experiences she's ever had. He's proven on numerous occasions that once two individuals become comfortable with each other, more than likely they will indulge in sexual activities despite any spiritual or other personal barriers. Carmelo's strategy remained the same, which was to have her remain calm and comfortable and being himself.

Belinda loved to talk, and he loved to listen. They would spend countless hours on the phone. She was actually the first person to describe Carmelo as articulate. A minimum of five hour conversations accrued on a nightly basis for three weeks straight before he was finally invited to her home. It was interesting to know that Belinda held numerous corporate positions for the government but was now only graduating from a junior college. After graduating high school, she jumped right into the workforce and excelled in every management position without obtaining a degree. Although she was ashamed of the moles on her face, Belinda was very beautiful. Her fair skin resembled Larraine's, but was a few pounds heavier. She was a healthy woman and did not drink, and her immaculate home was located in the Cheltenham section of the city. Carmelo surely upgraded as they would often meet in Germantown and drive around in her new Lexus. He didn't mind meeting her halfway due to the enormous expense for gas that summer. In the beginning it felt a little weird cruising around Melanie's neighborhood but that feeling eventually passed as they spent more and more time together. I precisely recall the first time that he paid her a visited. I gave him a ride after we finished dinner at a well-known Mexican Restaurant located in East Falls.

She was watering the lawn when I pulled in front of her home. Carmelo was excited, while she paced around the living room begging forgiveness for a messy coffee table. Creating sexual tension over the phone was the easy part, but now standing face to face was more dramatic for Belinda. She was in total disbelief that at age fifty, she was on the verge of sleeping with someone that was young enough to be her child. She finally calmed down and offered Carmelo something to drink, coincidentally both options of ice tea and Orange juice was his favorite beverages. He selected the ice tea and made himself comfortable on the couch and began flipping through the channels. He senses that she is stalling, and the spontaneous dice roller tosses the remote on the couch and frightens her by creeping up from behind. When she turns around, he slips his tongue inside her mouth leaving the ice completely melted that she previously held before his startling approach.

After the surprising gesture, he apologizes, which she doesn't object but escorts him back to the couch. He takes two sips and the harassment begins. Carmelo attacks her again, and touching her everywhere. She tries to resist but gives in and asks him to close the blinds. She then takes him by the hand and begins pulling him up the steps. Now it was Carmelo who was frightened when her dog begins growling viciously. She turns on the light in the middle room just to show Carmelo that the year old pit bull is in a cage. Her bedroom feels like a tundra due to extreme usage of the air conditioner. Implementing mind over matter Carmelo strips himself naked and pulls her on the bed. This was also sex education 102 for Carmelo regarding intercourse. He often experienced that Larraine and Adriane produced less moisture than the younger women he slept with, which caused him to excessively perform orally in order to continue the congenial moments.

He anticipated the same experience with Belinda, but he was completely wrong, as her love stream flowed like the Niagara Falls. Round two, three, four, and five were incredible. Belinda revealed to Carmelo that she hasn't been sexually active for thirteen years. It was extremely difficult to believe that this woman hadn't had sex in a little over a decade but, Carmelo slept with her in less than a month. He was good but we were a little skeptical about her integrity. All three of Carmelo's experiences with these women over all were similar, but the most dramatic difference about Belinda was that she was a coordinator for the Youth Ministry at her church. On the weekends she would specifically lecture to the young ladies about the dangers of unprotected sex and abusive relationships. Belinda even invited Carmelo to her church because she thought that he would be such a positive influence and a great role model for the young men who were at risk of becoming a menace to society.

Belinda had a sister that encouraged her relationship with Carmelo, calling it "A rebirth of her social life." But her twenty one year old daughter Hailey who recently moved out disliked Carmelo and made vague statements that he was taking advantage of her mother. Belinda only married her father because she found out that she was pregnant. And being the daughter of a pastor, and being only sixteen, that was the best alternative. The marriage was a complete nightmare. During their pillow talks Belinda would horrify Carmelo about how her ex-husband would beat and stab her at any given time. The most startling thing about her story was these horrific events took place in that same home. Her parents allowed her husband to move in until they found their own place. After it surfaced that her husband was having an affair she confronted his mistress, which led to her being beaten once he got home and saw the two women sitting in the living room. As men, sometimes we don't realize how much we tap into a woman's emotions just by looking directly into their eyes and listening to every word being mentioned. But Carmelo was only implementing what he was taught during his group class which was basic eye contact and great posture which are key in establishing trust.

It was impossible to heal the wounds of her traumatizing experiences, but Carmelo would offer his token of affection by taking her down to the museum water fountain to relax. At fifty years old, Belinda had never witnessed the romantic scene in the city due to her sheltered life style as a child and adulthood. It was simple genius by Carmelo! Being comfortable was the key. Belinda even allowed him to drive her Lexus as she rested her feet on the dashboard. It was a great summer and after spending two days with Belinda, Carmelo returned home to spend time with his family. He showered, poured a glass of wine and sat outside on his porch to catch the evening breeze. Calling Adriane wouldn't be a bad idea since he missed two of her phone calls during his getaway. She answers on the first ring and mentions that she is in the area. Her tax prepare lived around the corner from him and she had to pick up a few documents that she mistakenly left at his home office.

Carmelo was always a little weary of that relationship and joked about her sleeping with him although he was married with three children. She stopped by and they sat in her car and chatted for a while. She apologized again for missing his graduation and for them not being able to spend any time together due to her overwhelming work schedule. Even though his phone is on silent mode, he can tell that there are at least two missed phone calls from Belinda. He and Adriane decided to go out for pretzels and a water ice and spent the remaining of the evening at the neighborhood park until it was time for her to head back home and get dressed for work. We had about a week off until summer classes began and Carmelo spent each day going back and forth from his home to Belinda's house. One evening after sleeping the entire day at her place, he woke up in a pile of new summer outfits that were purchased from the Gap and old Navy. She suggests that a cruise around the city would be great after spending all day on her feet at the Cedar brook mall looking for his size.

They stopped at a neighborhood restaurant and ordered two signature salads and Buffalo wings to go. She directs Carmelo to a park that her mother seldom took her as a child. The Lakeview was beautiful as Carmelo just sat and listened to her reminisce about her childhood and how well the relationship had grown with her sister since the death of both of her parents, which took place during their twenties. Carmelo offers his gracious words of encouragement but is constantly interrupted by Hailey's crazy text messages and phone calls stressing that her mother is wasting her time and that there's no compatibility. Neither one of them is discouraged, in fact Hailey's behavior boost Carmelo's ego as he was infatuated with negative and positive attention. After finishing his salad, he offers Belinda the last buffalo wing from his plate. The gesture was portrayed in the movie "*The Brothers*", by the gorgeous, living legend, Jenifer Lewis. "After sharing a plate of food and if the man offers the woman the last bite then he was the right man for her." It was a symbol of the man not being a glutton and displaying generosity to his significant other.

Carmelo was just being generous he never got too caught up

in the Hollywood view of how to find true love. But his favorite theory was from the movie "A *Bronx Tale.*" The great Chazz Palminteri orchestrated finding your true love by "open your date's car door and while walking around to your side, watch carefully if she opens your door. If she does, she is the one. But if she doesn't you are to dump her and move on to the next one." This tactic would simply prove if a man was dealing with a selfish woman. Her daughter's text messages are relentless and Carmelo is now trying to figure out, who is the parent. They hit the road with him flying through every green light and enjoying the dynamic voice of the great Teddy Pendergrass. A long kiss good night is shared before she pops open the trunk so he can get his new outfits. Another kiss is shared before she departs. His neighbors stare in disbelief of how fortunate this young man is, and constantly has these older women flaunting over him.

Summer classes arrive, which Carmelo and I are looking forward to the land slide courses. Taking additional classes at CCP was less expensive and still would be transferable to our choice of university. I wasn't a huge fan of night school which began at five thirty and ended at eight, but since I worked during the day, it was the only option. For Carmelo it would be a simple task as he planned to sex Belinda into a coma, and sleep all day before heading to class. She used numerous sick days just to stay home with Carmelo. Belinda was really a great woman but within a couple of months into their relationship it became evident that Carmelo had laid it on a too thick. Concealing his listening and attentive manner would be the only way to tone things down between them. She had grown accustomed to having him sleeping over and holding her through the night. *And so could anyone that lived without sex for over a decade.* But it became overwhelming for Carmelo. She wanted him there every single day and night. After allowing me to listen to a voice message that she left, Belinda urged him to "Just stay right where you are, I don't care how far it is, I'll come and pick you up." At this time I didn't feel sorry for him. There were others who would love to be in this predicament. But as time went on, I ultimately began to feel his pain. One evening our professor was exhausted and decided to end class about a half hour early.

# Chapter 9
# Overdose

*Demoted Affection*

Carmelo and I attempted to cross Spring Garden Street to the Irish pub, but Belinda pulled directly in front of us. We just looked at each other and smiled, but there was absolutely nothing funny about the way this fifty year old was behaving. She became extremely possessive and questioned why Carmelo and I often chose the bar scene to hang out. When he tried to address the issue of him needing just a little space to relax, it led to a heated argument that resulted in him simply hanging up on her and going to bed angry. And of course she called back a million times and then accused him of seeing someone else. It was bad, but not chaotic. Truth be told, her house and car was worth a little frustration. It was due to the impact he had made on her. She was possibly falling in love with him, or simply just became addicted to his company. A few days passed and Adriane calls, to requests his presence for the upcoming weekend. Carmelo is revived but isn't in the mood for a getaway. So he just makes up an excuse about having to baby sit his little sister. There's actually some truth to his story because Carmelo is spending time with his daughter and has to pick her up in the morning. Belinda calls and presses the issue for him to spend the night with her and that she'll drop him off just in time to pick up his little girl. Although she had disclosed so much personal information, Carmelo didn't want her in his business.

The location where he had to pick up his daughter was dreadful. The nineteenth police district was no place for a child. However after considering how embarrassed he would be if she was to find out, he informed her about the bizarre arrangement. They arrived right on time, but are forced to wait an extra fifteen minutes until the little one is dropped off. When she arrived, the princess greets Ms. Simmons and takes liking to the luxurious vehicle. Belinda was appalled but remained very supportive during the uncanny ordeal. She takes Carmelo and his daughter straight home and wishes him a great weekend. The two days move by swiftly and Belinda has Carmelo held hostage back at her place. Although very annoying she was also very romantic. After he fixed her garage door that had been broken for the past five years, she lit some candles and poured scented baby oil in the tub and gave him a nice warm bath. She declined to join him, due to fear of over cooking the chicken parmesan that would include candle lights and a very expensive bottle of wine, which she surprisingly shared with him. The following night is similar, and Carmelo is flabbergasted that he might be getting out done by someone twice his age. Belinda informs him that the five rounds a night is a huge contribution to her great health. She suggest that maybe he should begin taking vitamins. He's slightly embarrassed and sarcastically replies "Vitamins, I don't need any vitamins to keep up with a senior citizen. I'll be fine just fine; I'll just start taking five minute breaks to be recharged." She hits him with a pillow but shortly after they fall asleep after watching the re-broad casting of the news.

Belinda and Carmelo really never went out as much, but when the nineteenth annual Jazz festival came to Ogontz Avenue. They were in attendance along with the other three thousand fans of Maze, The OJ's and The Whispers. It was the last night of the concert that Eden and I joined them before getting lost in the crowd. Belinda seemed a little shy about meeting us, but Eden soften her up by showing off his newly purchased portrait of Dr. Martin Luther King playing pool at a local lounge in Atlanta Georgia. Belinda still had family who lived in that area and the brief discussion of Dr. King made her feel comfortable hanging out with a bunch of twenty year olds. For the next few weeks everything ran smooth. Our classes were going well, and Belinda had calmed down tremendously. Carmelo and Adriane continued to rarely spend time together. They had strong feelings for each other but were temporally on different pages. Even though Carmelo never came clean about his relationship with Melanie and Belinda, Adriane knew that he couldn't go long without having sex. So there had to be someone in the picture that was satisfying him. But she really never pressed the issue about other women. Carmelo was young and around woman every day, the chances of him sleeping with another women was unquestionable.

Why question something that is more than likely to happen? But Carmelo's luck would soon run out. It was the end of the summer; he and I were successful and finished our courses with flying colors. I moved on to Drexel University but he chose to stay back for another year, taking additional classes that would make his time shorter after transferring to any prestigious university. Things also got a little sticky with him allegedly being spotted by some of Belinda's church members, rumors began to surface that a young man was entering her home after hours. This woman had a great reputation and was supposed to be setting the example for young people. When it was brought to her pastor's attention by an anonymous informant she denied any sexual activities took place. Her pastor insists that she dismiss Carmelo because their relationship was inappropriate and extremely disrespectful in the eyes of the lord. Carmelo and Belinda came to the conclusion that the evil deeds were done by her own daughter. Belinda was well respected by the members of her church and if it was someone else, they would have spoken to her in private. Hailey betrayed her mother out of spite because Belinda's world suddenly came to a pause when she met Carmelo. Belinda and Hailey were also best of friends. But like all relationships, the water began to run dry, and now that her mother was having some form of excitement in her life, Hailey couldn't stand the fact that, it was all about Carmelo.

She displayed pure hatred for Carmelo due to his age and never held a conversation with him. She also kept the pastor informed of her mother's disobedience as Belinda continued her affair with Carmelo. But it was pure genius on the pastors behalf, to have Belinda promoted to a full time position. She would be appointed head of the youth ministry. Instead of exposing her to the church and having her crucified for hypocrisy. He used Belinda for something positive by condemning her with the overwhelming position. The pastor also knew that Belinda was extremely blessed with being a nurturer, which would lead to a domino effect and this problem would be easily eradicated. After accepting the position, Belinda started to bring her work home, as she allowed some of the females from the ministry to come over during the week and even spend the night on the weekends. This was problematic for Carmelo and cutting his benefits. The Pastor's method worked brilliantly as Carmelo became frustrated. Spending time with Belinda overall was great, He didn't want to eliminate her, he just wanted things to cool down. Their quality time perished and he was now experiencing social neglect on both sides of the board from Adriane and Belinda. His run had finally come to an end and their last discussion took place in the middle of the night as Belinda informed him that one of the young ladies had moved in with her on a permanent basis. Neither one of them attempted to contact each other after hanging up, and Carmelo was provided with additional down time.

# Chapter 10
# Fresh Start

*Creating Memories*

It's the fourth of July weekend, and after a barbeque with my family, Carmelo remains with us while we head down to the Art Museum and enjoy the magnificent display of the fireworks. Surprise guest John Legend provided an exceptional performance and a lucky lady was swept off her feet when the R&B great pulled her on stage for a seductive serenation. In the middle of the concert Adriane texted to make dinner plans. He smiles and confirms that he would be free and would jump at her beckon call. For months he had pressed her about the tropical theme of Bahama Breeze where he and Melanie actually had their first official outing. A few days later Adriane got the chance to experience the Caribbean live music on the veranda dining room along with their martini specials. For his entertainment Carmelo begins teasing her, "I should really do a bit of research on what middle class professionals drink the most?" She's hammered and gives no response, but begins giving him sloppy kisses and apologizing for working like a slave. He interrupts her by mentioning "Look I know that I'm the best thing since slice bread, but your bills come first." A statement which vaguely rationalizes his behavior if she were to find out about his escapades, but which also is the truth concerning her financial obligations. Nevertheless she is determined to make it up to Carmelo and after dinner they head back to her place.

While he takes a shower, she decides to finally give Samantha a call, her former classmate from nursing school. A friendly conversation would be nice, as requesting a favor was Adriane's motive. She recalled Samantha's husband being an operations manager for a theme park but couldn't remember the exact one. So after about an hour of Samantha's slander session and filling her in on the latest gossip, Adriane's request is granted as Samantha rush delivers four tickets to Dorney Park. Everything went according to plan. The tickets arrived just before the weekend that Adriane was off. His little sister would certainly enjoy the day trip but Carmelo didn't hold his breath about his daughter joining them. Fortunately both girls were together and delighted when entering the park just before noon. They struggled to fine parking as you could imagine the huge crowd waiting to get on the extravagant roller coasters and chowing down on numerous plates of funnel cake. Carmelo immediately sets the ground rules." Stay close and don't even think about getting on one of those scary roller coasters." He thought that those who received any enjoyment out of getting on those rides, simply had some sort of death wish.

Every precaution would be taken pertaining to their safety. He was surely going to enjoy this beautiful outing with Adriane and the girls. Everything was perfect, the weather was great, there was more than enough to eat and plenty of photos were taken during the water rides. Adriane and Carmelo spent hours on the beach that was specially designed for the children while Tiara and Alissa played in the pool. He expresses his appreciation but is careful with his display of public affection in front of the little ones. As the night falls, Carmelo continues to relax while Adriane escorts the girls to the ladies room. He began packing their bags to leave, but once they returned the nagging began for one last ride. The Carnival lights were very enticing and Carmelo even joined them on the Mary go round, which was Adriane's favorite part of the evening. They loaded up and were on their way back home, with Adriane receiving much praise from the girls. Somehow she took a wrong turn, and ended up in Quaker Town.

The girls were fast asleep while Carmelo offered suggestions that were not beneficial in finding the correct way home. However Adriane implements the mentality of the Great Magellan and navigates her way back to the starting point and then returns everyone home safely. The girls quickly took a bath and headed off to bed. Carmelo then heads back outside for a recap of how much fun they had together. Adriane is exhausted, her eyes became heavy and she begins to sweat and mentions feelings of weakness in both arms and numbness in her legs. Carmelo quickly suggested that they head to the emergency room. They switch seats and head off to Lankenau Hospital. Right before pulling into the parking lot, he notifies his mother that he is still out but the girls are in his room sleeping. When he hung up the phone, it finally hits him that the chances of him running into Larraine have dramatically increased.

He begins to feel a little uneasy, while Adriane whispers to him that she is also feeling a little dizzy. There's no sign of Larraine at the registration counter. Adriane is in luck of not having to wait too long after she checks in with the intake clerk. There's a guy in the office that's being seen by the doctor. Carmelo can over hear him explaining the amount of pain in his right side after falling off a ladder on a construction site while working earlier that day. A little girl who sat directly across from Carmelo appears to be traumatized by a collision of her mother's car and an SUV. Both parties seemed to be fine, with the exception of the woman's car which was totaled. Carmelo hands Adriane a cup of water and begins to rub her face. The mother of the little girl begins to stare at Carmelo and is trying to figure out where they have met. The hallway begins to carry a familiar voice but Carmelo is distracted by comforting Adriane.

The little girl shouts "Grandma", Larraine appears and seconds later, a nurse calls for Adriane to enter the doctor's office. There all standing face to face, but Adriane remains in the dark about Larraine's existence. But for Larraine it's obvious who Adriane is, due to the affection that was being given to her by Carmelo. Confirmation is granted for Larraine's daughter and reminds her, that the baby is alright and was just a bit shaken up. Carmelo says "Hello" but Larraine does not respond. He senses that she is more shocked than angry, and he escorts Adriane into the doctor's office where he sits next to her attempting to avoid Larraine and any potential drama. The doctor then approached Carmelo and ask, "What is your relationship to the patient?", and they both respond that their just friends. Carmelo is asked to leave the office so that the doctor can perform a physical examination. He tries to avoid going back into the waiting area, so he heads to the men's room. He continues to stall by repeatedly brushing his hair and hopes upon returning, Larraine and her family would be gone. Sitting in the car would surely be an option but he considers what if Larraine begins her childish behavior and has a friendly conversation with Adriane and attempts to sabotage their relationship? About twenty minutes of contemplating whether to return back to the waiting room Carmelo puts an end to the nerdy school boy routine of hiding from his bullies in the bathroom and decides to face Larraine. He enters the waiting room and it's completely empty. He's not sure if Larraine is gone but heard some keys daggling around the corner by the snack machine. He does one last preparation in straightening his shirt and is ready for the confrontation. He takes a few extra steps, and it's Adriane buying him a bag of party mix. "Hey Handsome" She assumes that he went outside to wait in the car since it was a bit chilly in the lobby.

It was confirmed that Adriane was experiencing low blood pressure. She was given a prescription to receive some medication and told to take a couple days off. Three bags of party mix and two bottles of iced tea were purchased as they walked passed station number two, where Larraine was now sitting. Nothing was said, not a split second of eye contact was made. Larraine simply ignored them both as they walked out holding hands. Carmelo was not comfortable with Adriane driving all the way home, so they booked a hotel for the remaining of the night. The next morning Carmelo receives a phone call from his mother letting him know that the girls were up and driving her nuts. He gives her a promising "Ok, ok, I'm on my way", while Adriane is in the shower and has already ordered room service. He had no appetite for the large portion of French toast, turkey beacon, eggs with hash browns, so he requested a doggy bag. Adriane feels a whole lot better and quickly drops Carmelo off and returns home to follow the doctor's orders of getting some much needed rest. He opens the door and is tackled by the two little angels. His daughter gives him a guilty conscience by asking "Daddy where have you been? We woke up this morning and didn't see you" Carmelo is evasive and mentions "I brought breakfast for you guys" and reheats the uneaten meal that was intended for his delight.

His mother hurries off back to bed, leaving the girls under the control of their glorious idle. Carmelo checks the balance on his debit card and decides to take the little ones shopping for new clothes. After breakfast he insists that they clean their room and take a nap because he would be adding an extra treat. Carmelo had confidence that "*Madagascar 2*" starring Chris Rock and Ben Stellar would be a classic and wanted to catch the seven thirty show and the half off sale at Old Navy. After completing his laundry, he joined the girls for a nap, but right before he laid down, Adriane sent him a text message saying that she was also on her way to bed. After their nap, they all got washed, dressed and departed. Carmelo hadn't gone back to Old Navy since the day he met Larraine, and they finished up just in time for the movie. Marple shopping Center was crowded, but the day went according to plan. Chris Rock was hilarious and Carmelo took full advantage of the sale. He bought three outfits for both of the girls and continued the introductory stage of having them accustomed to nice things. When they returned home his mother was putting the finishing touches on supper. The aroma and site of the Velveeta cheese rice, with chicken and broccoli was great but quickly forgotten when the girls began their mini fashion show in trying on their new sun dresses. Carmelo then shouts up stairs for them to wash their hands and come down stairs for dinner. All praises are due to his mother for preparing the delicious meal.

The girls settled down for a late episode of "Jimmy Neutron", while Carmelo prepared a small bowl of mixed fruit for dessert. The peaches, apples and grapes are devoured by the girls like a pack of snarling wolves, but Carmelo finds great joy and pleasure satisfying their little cravings. He begins to doze off but his little sister taps him on the knee and shows him a text from Adriane. He replies just to make sure that she's alright, then continued to slouch on the love seat. The next morning his mother is up early again, preparing the girls for Sunday school. Carmelo decides to continue sleeping for a couple more hours and catch up with them for the afternoon service. It was actually his routine of arriving to church just in time for the day's message. Carmelo woke up to find the house completely empty as he expected, along with the sweet scent of his mother's perfume. It appears that the girls gave her a hard time due to the several different outfits lying across her bed. He checks his cell phone and saw that Adriane had

texted him "Good morning and to get up for church", he replied
back that he was on his way before getting into the shower. It's a
beautiful day in mid July, and he's press for time. He quickly irons
a casual shirt and slacks, checks his hair that resembles a tornado
and is out the door. The sixty five bus arrives right on time and
his Kenneth Cole fragrance is appealing to both male and female
passengers. Once he arrives in the lobby Carmelo is greeted by
the ushers for his presence.

He's well known throughout the congregation, and is spotted
by his sister who rushes over to him, heads turn to catch a glimpse
of the excitement as his daughter also follows. He made it just in
time to catch the guest speaker who delivered a powerful message
on temptation. After the hour sermon, Carmelo is filled with a
thousand blessings. His daughter is drenched with compliments
of how beautiful she is; while his attention is being sought by a
few of the young female members. Before jumping into the back
of his parents Ford Taurus, Carmelo shakes a few dozen hands
and waves goodbye as if he were running for president of the
United States. They head off to Grandpa Glenn's house, where
he would be delighted to have his great grandchildren join him
for Sunday dinner. Grandpa Glenn always prepared wonderful
meals and had been anointed the best cook in the family. The
collar greens, red beans and rice, fried chicken with onions and
gravy along with a fresh salad, fulfilled everyone's appetite after
a long day of worship.

When supper ended, Carmelo received another text message
from Adriane. It was unclear by what she meant, but the text
mentioned, going back to his roots. She sends another one,
requesting to pick him up after he drops his daughter off at the
police station. It's getting pretty late and they make plans to visit
Grandpa Glenn again next weekend. Carmelo and his family
pulls in front of the nine teeth police district where they wait
for about ten minutes until his daughter is picked up. He kisses

the princess and reminds her to do well in school. Once they arrive back home, he brushes his teeth and applies another dose of cologne on his wrist and waits for Adriane to call. He watched the ESPN high lights with his stepfather until his phone began to vibrate. Adriane arrived with a huge smile on her face. "What are you so happy about?", "Let's go somewhere quiet and I'll tell you all about it." Even though it appeared to be good news, Carmelo always thought of the worst case scenario. Her good news could mean bad news for him. They went to a twenty four hour diner in Manayunk and asked to be seated in the back, where they slid into a comfy booth and ordered some tea and shared a large portion of Crab fries.

Before their order had arrived Adriane blurted "I'm taking you to Jamaica for a week." Carmelo was speechless. He struggled with his words and began to stutter, "O wow, thank you, thank you very much, but what about work?" "I'm taking the doctor's orders and getting plenty of rest. A month ago I requested a one week, unpaid vacation and it was granted. This is your graduation gift. So are you coming or not?" Carmelo felt like trash because of his dealings with Melanie and Belinda, but he wasn't out of his mind. He went home that night and began packing. Carmelo didn't want to seem shallow by asking, how she could afford this expensive trip, especially during the peak season. But Adriane explained that two years prior to her meeting him, she was involved in a terrible car accident on her way to church. She was hit from behind which left her car totaled. After months of therapy she finally received a lump sum payment for an undisclosed amount. "I know that your mother and your daughter's birthday are in August and you probably would like to be here with them, so why don't we leave sometime next week? I planned for us to stay in the resort area and visit your birth place of St. Ann's Bay. He was thrilled, but also felt a little bad that he had to leave the girls and his parents behind. Nevertheless this would be a great trip for the both of them. It was perfect timing, as the summer was closing, because once August arrives it's pretty much back to work and preparing for school. Even though they had been seeing each other for months, this would probably be a good time to introduce Adriane to his parents. Their title was still up in the air, but at least his parents would know who their son was leaving the country with. So before leaving the diner Carmelo makes this suggestion and Adriane quickly agrees.

The next day he informed his parents about the trip that Adriane had planned for him and that she would be stopping by to meet them. They were happy for Carmelo; he needed to be reacquainted with his birthplace, while enjoying the site of those beautiful Jamaican women. Later that evening Adriane stopped by and his mother welcomes her with a glass of iced cold lemonade. Shortly after his father walks in adjusting his glasses, and says "Hello." Adriane then pulls out her laptop and shows his parents a few pictures of the hotel and the resort area. They planned to leave about a week later but a terrible storm had just ripped through Kingston and was threatening other areas where they planned to stay. Even though their tremendously disappointed, Adriane suggest that they go to Bermuda instead of taking a huge risk of having their vacation ruined. She immediately informed Southwest Airlines of the sudden cancelation to the beautiful island, which actually works in her favor.

The young man who worked as a sales representative was possibly motivated to go beyond the call of duty when hearing Adriane's seductive accent when requesting two tickets for the resort area. He offered her a generous discount, and apologized for any inconvenience that the storm had caused. Struggling to decide what outfits to choose, Carmelo had packed almost a month's worth of clothes, as Adriane booked the first early morning flight to Bermuda. A few days later they met up at Philadelphia International Airport at six am, which the big day came instantly as Carmelo was filled with excitement and had difficulty sleeping that night. Adriane was already there sitting in the lobby eating a sausage and cheese sandwich. The last time that Carmelo traveled on a plane, he was eleven years old. His entire family and a host of friends went to Jamaica for his parents wedding. For Adriane it has only been a few years since her last flight, but it wasn't a pleasant trip, as she returned home to bury her beloved mother.

# Chapter 11
# Welcome to Bermuda

*High jacking the heart*

They arrived at the airport about forty five minutes before departing. It's just enough time to make a bathroom run and purchase a few snacks before heading back. They say a quick prayer and seconds later, their flight number is called. They begin boarding the plane and Carmelo attempts to make Adriane's flight more enjoyable by offering her the widow seat. He kisses her again and thanks her for taking him on what will surely be the time of his life. His new iPod is irrelevant as he quickly falls asleep, once they got comfortable. She then makes use of his album selection while the plane begins to take off. The Captain wishes everyone a safe flight and within minutes, the two hundred passenger bird rips through the clouds. They reach Bermuda international airport within four hours. Carmelo is impacted by the raging sun light, but he's actually blinded by the women strolling around in their bikinis.

Adriane checked to make sure that they had all of their

belongings, while Carmelo called his parents to let them know that they had arrived safely. The luggage staff welcomes them and mentions that they arrived just in time for the big music festival that would be taking place not too far from their hotel. They made a quick stop at a local grocery store and headed straight to their hotel suite that had a gorgeous ocean view. The people of Hamilton, Bermuda had a soft accent with exotic features. Carmelo was well rested from sleeping the entire trip, and surprisingly Adriane wasn't tired and suggested that they have brunch at the beach restaurant across the boardwalk. The food was delicious and similar to the Jamaican West Indies cuisine. After a long day and having three entrees, they both were now exhausted. The next morning Carmelo awakes very early, a group of birds fly pass the orange sun in their well-known skein formation. He then spots two lovers enjoying a stroll on the beach. Although standing from a distance, Carmelo can still see the young woman smiling from ear to ear. She resembles the beautiful and talented Gabrielle Union, but something strange is occurring. Carmelo begins to wonder, why they would stop directly in front of his window. The young man took her by the hand and got on one knee. Carmelo was tempted to wake Adriane but figured in a weird sense that it would sound better as a story. The young lady covered her mouth, more than likely to prevent herself from waking up those who like to sleep at six am. She couldn't help weeping and suddenly began screaming "Yes, I do, I, do." Afterwards they began jumping around and ran into the ocean. It was a beautiful sight, rather perfect as Adriane woke up and asked Carmelo what was he thinking about?

He just smiled and replied "Nothing." She then mumbled that he should come back to bed because it was still early and they had plenty of time until the festival began. He remained glued to the window and couldn't help the thought of him and Adriane walking on the beach during the early morning or perhaps a romantic sunset, and then asking her to marry him. It was without a doubt that he had very strong feelings for Adriane and she felt the same, but the cons certainly outweighed the pros. His career was in shambles and he was still in the process of completing his education. But the million dollar question was, Could he submit to fidelity for the rest of his entire life? Carmelo was more concerned with having financially stability. He did recall the conversation that they had in the car on New Year's night, which Adriane mentioned that one day she would like to be married but was unsure if she wanted anymore children. He then made a cup of hot chocolate to distract himself from the ironic thoughts. But a more vivid picture was formed when he realized that it probably wouldn't be a bad idea to elevate their relationship because he also doubted wanting any more children. While sitting on the love seat, it dawned on him that he was just getting caught up in the moment and was overreacting to the romantic scene by the newly engaged couple.

Carmelo was a philosopher at heart, so he began contemplating that this vacation could create a new found perspective on their relationship. They were certainly compatible, but what would Adriane think of being engaged to him in this short period of time? It had been less than a year since they've been dating, but of course felt much longer. He saw her squirming around and quickly made a second cup of hot chocolate along with two scrambled eggs and sausages. "Good morning beautiful", "Wow breakfast in bed, thank you sweetie." She finished breakfast, but morning sex causes them to over sleep and to almost miss the festival. After pealing themselves off each other, the sun was already at its peak and the festival was well underway. They both showered and wore Jamaican t-shirts with cargo shorts. More time is wasted as Carmelo can't find his sneakers but finally decides to wear his sandals which feel more comfortable than his cross trainers. Adriane brought along her new digital camera and

Carmelo finally made use of his binoculars that was given to him for his twenty first birthday by his uncle Pete. It was now in the afternoon and Carmelo flagged down a cab that carried them into the town of St. George's. Shockingly! The streets were not packed until the driver mentioned that he'd taken a short cut to avoid traffic. Carmelo gives the cab driver a generous tip for a job well done as they have a clear view of the festival. It was a wonderful experience as local singers opened the show for a few U.S artists. Carmelo encouraged Adriane to join him in getting her face painted. "I look ridiculous she whispered" and tried to cover her face, which caused the butter fly painting to smear. Carmelo thought it was hilarious and took pride in his dragon decoration. They took pictures and purchased key chains, stuff animals and coffee mugs for souvenirs. Afterwards they bought fish platters from a dinner truck and sat in the grass enjoying the great sounds of the Caribbean music. It was a great day and everything was perfect, which only made thoughts of settling down with Adriane reappear. The festival was now ending and they began to make their way back to the hotel. Once they got back, Carmelo had begun storing away the souvenirs, while Adriane dominated the bathroom scrubbing her face. It was still early but they couldn't decide whether to stay in, or to go out for dinner.

Carmelo fell asleep on the love seat watching television, as she lied across the bed with the balcony doors open and welcoming a pleasant breeze. Carmelo awoke and stood over her as she slept peacefully. Her long silky hair covered her face which he gently removed and softly kissed her cheek. She awakened and held him tightly, with no words being said. Carmelo's deep breath and kiss on the forehead is piercing and she leaps out of bed into the bathroom and begins bushing her teeth. She returns and mentions that they should go out for dinner and try the jerk chicken at a nearby Caribbean restaurant. A co-worker had recommended that she try the restaurant whenever visiting St. George's. Carmelo ignores her actions and avoids having a discussion about their feelings and plays along. His blue Armani pants are chosen along with an olive green shirt that went perfect with his dark brown Steve madden sneaker shoes. Carmelo had always had great taste in fashion and decides to try his luck by requesting to choose Adriane's dress for the evening. He selects a violet red dress from Donna Karen along with matching shoes. He then begins to search through her suitcase for her Chanel perfume, which is already on the night stand. Adriane remained doing her hair in the bathroom. The fabric for her dress required minimum heat, so to save her time; he begins to iron her dress. She returns from the steamy room and is exceptionally pleased with his choice. "Now that's sexy, and just the way you make me feel, thank you sweetie."

He attempted to iron his clothes but was extremely distracted when she began applying a touch of baby oil on her breast and then working her way down her legs. A fierce eye connection is made; Carmelo removed the ironed clothes and then threw her on the bed. She playfully tries to resist, but gives in once he begins to taste her. It was getting pretty late but they hurried back into the shower, got dressed and were out the door. They got outside just in time to catch the cab as another couple was leaving. "Where to" the driver shouted in his heavy accent. Adriane mispronounced the name of the restaurant, which was "The Courto." But the driver immediately corrected her and stated that he had just left there and was dropping off the other couple. He continued to rave about the restaurant, calling it one of the best in town and before losing his management position at a production company, he used to take his ex-wife there all the time. Carmelo utters to the driver that "Maybe you should have changed restaurants." His joke landed smoothly and the trio enjoyed the humorous gesture before heading into the restaurant.

Fortunately they were seated next to the water fall view. "What a beautiful sight, isn't it Carmelo?" "It's absolutely gorgeous, but nowhere close to you. Adriane I'm not sure if its love, but my feelings have changed for you and I've been feeling this way for some time now. I truly think that this trip was supposed to happen so that I could have the perfect opportunity, in a setting like this, to let you know exactly how I feel even though you might not feel the same". She's speechless; in fact she nearly chokes on the glass of ice water. She prepares to offer a response but is interrupted by the waitress. She orders the jerk chicken, rice and beans with a side of cabbage. Carmelo orders the same with a glass of wine, while she gathers her thoughts. She clears her throat with expectations of confidence in replying to Carmelo's heartfelt sincerity. She begins to stumble over her words and Carmelo just sits there with a smirk on his face. "Wow, I'm sorry Carmelo I'm just a little surprised, but to be honest I feel the same way about you. And I agree with you that the feelings are strong, but maybe a little short of love. But let's face it pretty boy, your basically pushing thirty. It's either we're going to be in a committed relationship or not. I'm not worried about your current financial status because that's only temporary. The first thought I get that you're trying to use me, I'll simply kick you to the curve and easily have you replaced by one of the few dozen men that have been showing a general concern for my best interest.

This is certainly not about money Carmelo, because if you stay in the Behavior Health field, my taxes would be in the same bracket as your net income. It's you that I care for. I'm also not concerned about your possible flings with other women during our rough patch because I myself was not ready to make a full commitment. But it's such a relief that we can express our true feelings and share this moment together." Completely shocked out of his mind to see her sternness, but relieved that she's not troubled by the whoring, he concedes. "You know what you're exactly right, and I would certainly love to begin a fresh start with you." They both begin to notice the weird looks from the other diners which gave Carmelo a rush. He then decides to have a little fun by asking one of the waiters to take pictures of them kissing and feeding each other. It was obvious that the entire room was skeptical of their relationship so they just continued with their antics. After dinner they both agreed that the chicken was extremely spicy but delicious.

Midnight was approaching but neither of them was in a hurry to get back to the hotel. Before leaving to go to the water fall that also had a miniature golf course, Carmelo orders two peach pies with strawberries and whip cream. Adriane doesn't complete her meal and ask for a doggy bag. Carmelo pays the check and they head off to the jungle like atmosphere. While caressing each other and enjoying the calm breeze, Carmelo notices the couple from the beach and enlightens Adriane that the gentleman's proposals was flawless. She places her head on Carmelo's shoulder as he continued to tell her that it was because of their moment of grace, which inspired him to inform her, of his true feelings. It was the most romantic place either of them had ever witnessed but they were soon joined by other couples from the restaurant. Adriane took pictures of Carmelo standing in front of the waterfall as he continued to stuff his face with desert. A playful Carmelo then decorates her nose with a little whip cream and snaps her picture, which she immediately erased.

Suddenly, it was like they saw their reflection in the mirror as well as a strange sense of competition. A young man that appeared to be around Carmelo's age respectively approached and asked "Could either of you be so kind and take a picture of me and wife?" Carmelo assisted the honey mooners in captioning their Kodak moments while Adriane admired how supportive he was in assuring that others would also reminisce about the illustrious vacation. After taking several photos of the couple, they introduced themselves and got to know each other pretty well. Jared and Yvette Wallington were from Peoria, Illinois. They were celebrating their second anniversary and enjoying their last week in a family owned villa. It was like two singles having an instant connection but instead all four were a perfect match. Jared was a twenty seven year old communication specialist for Verizon, while Yvette was forty two and worked as a stenographer for the municipal courts.

Carmelo was very embarrassed to mention that he was receiving unemployment, so he quickly changed the subject to how well he thought their pictures would turn out, until Jared redirected the conversation and asked "So what is your profession Carmelo?" Carmelo was always crafty, even when being nervous and giving a response. He simply replied that he worked in a youth detention center for three years and that's where he and Adriane met. Jared and Yvette also had a one year old son by the name of Tyler. They found a nice picnic area and listened to the story of how they both met three years ago. It was during a fundraiser that her family was hosting for breast cancer awareness month. Jared had just graduated from Pittsburgh University and made a huge donation for the worthy cause. When he first asked her out, she thought he was out of his mind until she was actually persuaded by her girlfriends. Their story was cut short by a slight drizzle, so they switched phone numbers and made dinner plans. The guys manage to flag down two cabs and went their separate ways with high expectations of continuing the cordial acquaintance.

While it was clear that Yvette was a very beautiful brunette with a tan that would probably last in the winter. During the cab ride back to the hotel, Adriane struggled to figure out Jared's nationality due to his light features and brownish hair, but Carmelo made it clear that he was a black man. "Those two are really something" Adriane mentioned while laying on Carmelo's chase. "Was it just me or did they make you feel a little jealous?" Carmelo answered nonchalantly "No, not really it was more inspiring than jealousy. It's actually confirmation and great to see that two mature adults despite their age difference take the next step in their relationship." Confirmation indeed, Adriane wasn't exactly sure what Carmelo was pushing for but felt as though he wanted more from her and perhaps she wanted more from him. They both were playing it cool and trying not to feel pressured by Jared and Yvette. She was glad that they had finally made their status official at dinner. It was his ambition that she was securing by not hastily submitting to what was truly a wonderful thought of being Carmelo's wife. Adriane wanted the best for him, and that was for Carmelo to stay focus on his education and career.

If implemented correctly he would be three times the man that he already was. But of course the thought of her robbing him of his youthful experiences continued to wonder in her mind. More sleep was needed as touring the city of Hamilton was on their agenda before catching up with Jared and Yvette for dinner later that evening. While snuggling up next to each other after their shower together, Adriane couldn't help asking Carmelo "Do you think anything went wrong with their baby, or at least in her mind?" because she did have him at a late age. "I don't know, but I'm sure you ladies will get all the details about each other's personal lives tomorrow at dinner," "Come on Carmelo", "Well it's the truth, but wait a minute, so you were jealous of Yvette and Jared?" "Ok maybe I was a little jealous of them. But that's only because I do see us when looking at them, and the newly engaged couple you pointed out to me. But what's most important is how much of an impact we've had on each other."

"I won't pretend like the thought of you one day being my wife has not crossed my mind once or twice, maybe three or four times." She playfully begins to mock his indirect proposal, "Well look whose getting caught up in the moment, because I know that those thoughts haven't crossed your mind while in cold ass Philadelphia." After speaking from the heart with so much fire and compassion. The exchange of such intense words led to exhilarating sex under the pale moon light that was accompanied by the sound of the ocean tides. The next morning Adriane woke up leaving Carmelo scrambling for pillows to block out the sun light. She had showered and packed enough food that would last throughout the day. She then awakened the young King with a kiss on the lips while adjusting her tone, to the mode of a drill sergeant. With his ears ringing, Carmelo noticed that she had already chosen his clothes for the day and laid them out on the love seat. As usual, she was holding the bathroom hostage. He just took another glance at the navy blue swim trunks and pink t- shirt and went back to bed.

She repeats herself several times for him to get up but is ignored. She then walks over and begins to pull the covers off Carmelo and sprinkling water on him. He wipes his face, and begins throwing the pillows at her before finally getting up and showering. While touring the city of Hamilton they visited a few historical sites. There first stop was the St. Peter's Church that was built in 1612. Afterwards they stopped by the Bermuda National Trust Museum that was built in 1700. And finally a court house that was built in 1917, unfortunately it was prohibited to take any photographs of the facilities.

# Chapter 12
# Something to prove

*Proper Placement*

The weather was amazing. Young children were laughing and playing in the streets.

Adriane made it noticeable that she and Carmelo were tourist by making extreme usage of her camera once leaving the historical sites. They were constantly approached by local civilians selling some pretty good merchandise. However no chances were taken on purchasing the possible stolen goods and Carmelo opted for a little boy sitting on the curb with a bucket of roses and cashews. He bought a rose for Adriane and a bag of peanuts for himself. They took a break at an Ice cream parlor and shortly after she received a call from Yvette to confirm their dinner plans for later that evening. Adriane had invited them to their beach restaurant because a well-known Caribbean band was scheduled to perform at seven o'clock. They had gotten back to the hotel around four, and had plenty of time until Jared and Yvette had arrived. Carmelo relaxed and took it easy on the balcony smoking a cigar, while Adriane remained inside preparing for competition. Immature thoughts began to lurk in her mind that wearing similar colors would symbolize to Jared and Yvette, or at least promote her status with Carmelo to more than just dating. She chose a cranberry shirt for Carmelo with blue slacks along with her mini burgundy skirt with a sexy split that was sure to turn heads, but not making Carmelo uncomfortable as he looked forward to the boat load of compliments.

He returns from the balcony, laughing and shaking his head. "Wow it seems that I wasn't the only one that was inspired by our rivals, but we're certainly the hottest couple on the island." "I just thought it would be cute, so get dressed, I don't want to keep them waiting." Carmelo is in and out of the shower, he gets dressed and returns back to the balcony. Adriane is dolled up, and adds her last coat of lip stick. Carmelo walks back into the room and is amazed. "Now I believe in God. "Adriane is looking rather radiant and prepared to put her competitors to shame. They got down stairs just as Jared and Yvette walked through the double doors of the lobby. "Excellent choice of colors" Yvette raved, and reminded Adriane that her dress resembled the one that Michelle Obama wore the night Barack won the presidential election. Adriane feels a slight blow to her intent to be original, but remains silent due to the glorifying comparison between her and the first lady.

Yvette's all black mini skirt and yellow top with heels gives her the appearance of a twenty year old. The two pharaohs escort their queens across the board walk and making no stops to the restaurant. They momentarily wait to be seated as Adriane's dress strikes the attention from an all guy's table. Of course this is quite normal, but one joker decides to continue staring so Carmelo removes his palm from Adriane's hips and provides the idiot with a better view. Jared smiles at Carmelo and joins the tension by fondling Yvette. Carmelo continues his taunts by winking his eye as they are now being seated. The Caribbean band set the mood along with the scented candle lights. Their waitress, who was a young Asian woman places menus and four glasses of ice water on the table and gives them time to order. Jared and Yvette constantly express their gratitude for the kind gesture. Their appreciation was a little overwhelming, but gave Adriane the opportunity to finally come clean and mentioned that they were such an inspiration to her and Carmelo in wanting to take their relationship to the next level. While deciding what to order, Adriane added that "It was the least thing that we could do since it was your anniversary." That surely didn't help Yvette's emotions as she began to sob and blowing her nose.

The waitress returns and Yvette pulls herself together and they all ordered the red snapper with rice and fried plantains. Apple and Strawberry martinis were requested afterwards to mellow out the night. Jared then stated the obvious "We're not the best Christians, and suggested that putting God first in their marriage and having as much fun as possible was the key to their marriage. "Continue getting to know each other and expect nothing, but enjoy everything you both share. But just like any other experience, communication is the vitally important. Yvette and I wanted to have children and we were blessed with a healthy baby boy." Yvette then chimes in by showing pictures of baby Tyler having his first birthday party. Carmelo spoke briefly about his daughter, with Adriane mentioning that her son was several years younger than Carmelo. Dinner arrives and the steaming fish is glowing with the light butter sauce.

Both couples join hands as Jared enforces a dominating role, but in a respectful manner and says grace. This gives Carmelo a blow to his ego, it's nothing dramatic but he begins to wonder if Adriane is admiring Jared's charming manner. After a few more sips of his martini, he catches himself being pathetic and realizes that all respect is due to the man of the hour. He praises Jared on a job well done with a simple handshake when the ladies tuned them out for a more in-depth discussion about each other's hair and fingernails. The music is paused as the bands takes a bathroom break. Carmelo isn't satisfied with his childish emotions and goes the distance by requesting for the attention of the entire restaurant and announces that Yvette and Jared were celebrating their second anniversary. Completely shocked, Yvette covered her face in attempt to avoid any further embarrassment. They received a standing ovation, and minutes later three bottles of champagne were sent over from the all guys table. It was a sincere notion from the gentlemen because they had already established their entertainment for the night with a few ladies from a bachelorettes party. The bottles of Champagne were tucked away by Jared and the ladies ordered a second round of martinis. The waitress returns with the desert menu and the strawberry banana cake is pleasing for the ladies but the guy's ordered another round of drinks and begun their predictions on who would win the Super bowl.

# Chapter 13
## Stronger Love

*No Competition*

J ared and Yvette were extremely happy and had recently purchased their first home together. It was a single four bedroom room house that was advertised on a foreclosure list. Jared was precise in revealing that at first his parents were totally against him dating Yvette, after all she was old enough to be his mother. Yvette's younger sister Sharlet, who was only thirty years old at the time, felt a little jealous that Jared showed absolutely no interest in her despite being closer to his age. Sharlet resembled one of the Kardashian sisters and was drop dead gorgeous, but came with a boat load of baggage that included three children from a previous relationship. The drinks were now starting to kick in as Jared continued to rant about their marriage "We complete each other, but know when to give each other a little space. And that's when our finish basement comes in very handy. I often go down there to relax, maybe call over a couple of friends, have a few beers and listen to some music. I had a personal bathroom installed and that's where her therapy sessions are usually held.

It's getting pretty late, but they all remain seated finishing up desert. Jared and Yvette are once again congratulated by other diners who have decided to call it a night. Adriane's suggestion of going for a brief stroll before going their separate ways is declined by Carmelo. "I'm certainly in no shape to go anywhere accept across that board walk and into my bed." Jared and Yvette both agree that it would not be safe, so Adriane pays the check and make their way back to the hotel. The two beautiful women wait patiently as their handsome soldier's flagged down a cab. The cool breeze had blown away Carmelo's buzz but after waiting a few minutes a cab arrived. Instead of walking back to the hotel, they just rode back with Jared and Yvette. Before leaving Jared gave Carmelo a bottle of Champagne and invited him for a round of golf. The next morning Carmelo and Adriane slept until midday due to their wrenching hang overs. However Carmelo was awakened by a telephone phone call from his mother, just to check up on him and Adriane and to see if their having a great time.

His voice was scruffy and he spoke with a slur. Apparently his brain cells had not yet awakened but Adriane finally did when he slammed the phone back on the hook. He lays in bed and stairs at the balcony doors. He's fascinated by the seagulls soaring high in the sky and on the hunt for their next meal. A long yawn and a stretch is released before getting up and taking a warm shower. Adriane remains sleeping, while he made a cup of tea and sat on the balcony. The surfers were quite entertaining as well as the young ladies who sun tanned on the beach. After finishing his tea, Carmelo got dressed and went for a stroll on the beach. Adriane remained out of character and sleeping her life away. She was in no shape to join him and neither did he want her company at this time. It was a moment to reflect on his thoughts that were similar to the ones during the early morning stroll of the newly engaged couple. Over and over again, he asked himself the same question. "How long can I continue this lifestyle without being able to commit to one woman"?

His feet sinks into the warm sand with the breeze blowing his linen shirt exposing the six pack that he ardently maintained. He recalls his older brother Shannon informing him at age fifteen that "Carmelo you should always feel as though you can get any woman you want." This token was certainly a huge contribution that ignited his promiscuous manner. Paranoia began to surface as he began to wonder if he was making the correct choice in investing all his time with Adriane and feared heartbreak. Carmelo was only in his mid-twenties and if he did decide to have any more children, Adriane would be pushing fifty. The question of her health possibly failing was relevant due to the fact that he would face the extreme barriers of being a single parent. So was it actually meant for Carmelo to marry an older woman? Or were these life experiences being taught through sporadic relationships? Did Adriane really want Carmelo to focus on his education and career, just for her own financial security before making their status official? And if that's the case, what happened to "For better or for worse?"

This certainly was not a one sided issue, they both had valid reasons for possibly remaining skeptical of the success of their relationship. The typical woman her age would gladly accept a relationship with such a bright and gorgeous young man. Despite all his attributes, Adriane probably thought she could do better and was holding off until she found Carmelo Johnson in someone around her age. What if all the time invested in their relationship did result in them getting married? Her son who adored and was very protective of her could possibly create conflict like Belinda's daughter. How would she handle any conflicts between the two kings who would now share the thrown of being in constant need for her affection? He's distracted by the young ladies playing volley ball in their bikinis. A Frisbee came flying in his direction, which he catches and hands back to a woman that resembled a swimsuit model.

Carmelo seemed to be maturing by the hour, and the trip did actually set his spirit free that marriage would be in his near future. He was destined to have everlasting love, but also came to the conclusion that it did not have to be with Adriane. Carmelo continued a monogamous relationship with her and of course implemented the advice of Jared in keeping great communication. He would not hesitate to inform Adriane that it was time for them to go their separate ways. Life was just too short to commit all, or even a little time into a sham. He walks further into the ocean to clear his mind of skepticism, disappointment and the recovery stage of a possible disaster. He's knee deep, and his reflection appears in the blue salt water and shortly after so does Adriane's. Her hair is in a ponytail and she looks fresh out of high school. She begins smiling and posing in her yellow bikini with red polka dots. They begin splashing each other and she runs toward the beach for safety. She's gently tackled by her young lover in the sand while others nearby find amusement in their romantic ruff housing.

After cleaning themselves off, their asked by one of the young ladies to join her friends for another round of volley ball. Carmelo quickly accepts, and jumps to his feet while pulling Adriane by the hand, and they both enjoy the thrill of a little friendly competition. Amazingly! Adriane did pretty well, she was great in the bed, but witnessing her athleticism was truly a new experience. So after an hour of jumping around with a bunch of twenty year olds, she was in desperate need of a massage. Her age began to show when limping back to the hotel. The sun is setting with the sky transforming into three different colors. On their way back, Carmelo steps around a pile of sea shells but stops to collect a few that looks unusual and what may have extraordinary value. Adriane observes one and confirms how incredible it looks, but is uncertain about the shells quality. For Carmelo, he wishes that it was his moment of proposing to her. His mentality is advanced, his physical appearance is phenomenal, the setting is perfect but his timing is off. They know exactly what's on each other's mind but remain silent. She gazes into his eyes and embraced him with a soft kiss. Carmelo then stores the shells into her pouch and they continue holding hands while making their way back to the hotel

They took a shower together and afterwards Carmelo thoroughly rubbed her down from head to toe with a heavy dosage of baby oil. She eventually fell asleep leaving Carmelo with a huge appetite. Room service would be perfect as he was now exhausted. He places two orders of turkey sandwiches and lemonade which surely boosted his energy. After his early dinner, Adriane remained sleeping, so he hit the beach again and joined his new friends playing football. He was having the absolute time of his life. But after just one session everyone departed. He returned to see Adriane glued to one of her favorite novels. "Hey there handsome, you surely got plenty of exercise today", "So did you gorgeous, you were trying to put me to shame out there." "Yes, I enjoyed myself but I sure paid for it, and thank you for the massage. You saved me two hundred dollars for a spa treatment." "You're welcome beautiful, so would you like the happy ending?" "Sure, why not?" She then places the fiction drama story under her pillow and marinates in the reality of Carmelo's true love. The next morning Adriane jumps up and calls Yvette. She almost forgot that their vacation ended the same time, with less than a couple of days remaining. She thought that inviting them over for brunch would be a good idea but Carmelo thought that she was over doing it.

"They seem really great Adriane but their celebrating their anniversary. So it's safe to assume that they would like to spend the last couple of days alone?" "Your right but, didn't Jared invite you to play golf with him?" "Yes he did, but since I don't even golf, I wouldn't bother wasting his time." Adriane is determined and still makes the phone call. Jared answers on the first ring, and she immediately begins to apologize for possibly interrupting an intense moment. But Jared gives a similar Carmelo response and informs her that everything is cool, their just relaxing and taking it easy. He hands the phone to Yvette and she's pleased to hear from her. She mentions to Adriane that they already have plans for the day, but tomorrow would be much better. In fact Yvette invited them over to the Villa and mentioned that they would love to spend their last day with them. Adriane doesn't argue with Yvette's generosity but just grasp on to the many qualities that they both have in common besides being involved with men young enough to be their children. They all agree that twelve thirty the next day would be great. Carmelo studies the clouds and it began to rain, which would have ruined the sumptuous lunch he wanted to have on the balcony, so he spent the rest of the day ordering room service and demolishing Adriane's vagina. Its ten o'clock the next morning, the rain has passed but the skies remain gray. Adriane is up and ready for their date with her idols. She allows Carmelo to sleep as she watches the forecast for the rest of the day. An hour later she yanks his pillow and begins tickling his feet, which dissects any thought of returning back to bed. He adds a burgundy cardigan sweater with a t-shirt and khaki shorts that she chose for him and they arrive on time to meet Jared standing in the driveway. They entered the luxurious living room that exposed a garden view, and Yvette is adding her last coat of lipstick before leaving the master bedroom.

Everyone, except for Carmelo enjoyed Yvette's egg omelet and sausages along with a cup of coffee. He advised everyone that a trip to the emergency would ruin the day, as he was allergic to eggs. Yvette apologizes and offers to make him something else but he denies and simply has the sausages and orange juice. Adriane and Carmelo began to express how much they admired their refined vocation home. It resembled a mini mansion, which the bathroom provided a view of the golf course. Jared was no pro, but boasted that he would be teaching Carmelo a thing or two after eating. Even though Carmelo didn't tell Jared that he wasn't much of a golf player, he figured that it would be a perfect time for some male bonding. Carmelo learned a lot from Jared, but learning how to play golf would be the least. Getting a few more pointers from Jared would only improve his pursuit to being established with Adriane. A few seconds of uneasiness surfaces due to this being the last day remaining on Jared and Yvette's vacation. And it escalates when Adriane bails out on Carmelo by asking to go to the ladies room. Brunch is almost finish and they all wait until Adriane returns, which she does in minutes with a factious smile that only Carmelo catches. Her unsteady behavior continues to be unnoticed due to Yvette being such a wonderful hostess. Adriane then requests a second cup of coffee to calm her nerves. Carmelo continues to observe her unusual vibe and is quite baffled. He even tunes Jared out, when asked "So what college are you planning on completing your degree?" Carmelo returns to earth just in time to answer "Sure, why not" when Jared mentions that it's time to hit the golf course. Kisses are shared by both couples and the guys make their way to the course. As soon as the door closes behind them, Yvette turns to Adriane and asks "Are you alright?" Apparently as a woman, she picked up on the same vibes that Carmelo did. "I didn't want to ask you in front of the guys and make you feel uncomfortable." "Everything is fine, I just haven't been getting enough sleep lately", "I'm way ahead of you, that's one of the disadvantages of dealing with these younger men."

They both laughed as Adriane accepts another omelet with orange juice. She stresses to Yvette that "I really haven't been feeling well for the past couple of weeks but I couldn't cancel the trip. I really wanted to do this for Carmelo. He and I really needed this vacation." Yvette was very attentive, but the truth about Adriane's condition was more appropriate for Carmelo to know first, or at least to him, that would be more realistic. But no man's ego can stop two women with an instant connection. After taking the last bite of her omelet Adriane finally came clean and told Yvette that she was pregnant. Yvette is excited but maintains low tones when uttering "I knew it; you had the same look on your face when I stared in the mirror for about an hour after finding out that I would be in my forties and having my first child. I remember how I tried my best to act normal but my little sister knew that I was pregnant before I could say the words."

Yvette apologizes for rambling and allows Adriane to express her feelings. "I never had plans to have children at this age. Carmelo is in college, and already has a daughter who he is struggling to take care of. I'm also not married, dating is one thing, but having this young man's child is another. Nevertheless his mother would surely believe that I was trying to ruin him. Truthfully Yvette, I already have my mind made up that I am not going to bring a child into the world under these circumstances." "So what's Carmelo going to say?" "I don't know, but I do know that he's in love with me. It's written all over him, he really hasn't figured it out yet, but he wants to take our relationship to the next level. We never really discussed having a child together." While Yvette asked opened ended questions it was unclear to Adriane whether she was trying to persuade her to keep the baby or was just being nosey. Yvette continued to play therapist by asking "Do you love him?" she replied yes but I'm not having his child under these circumstances.

He's still a young man with a bright future, the less distractions he has, the more successful he will become." "Well right now you're speaking for Carmelo. Sit him down and tell him everything that you just told me, but don't be surprised if he doesn't agree with you. Adriane, this is your first experience being involved with a younger guy and it's clear that Carmelo is very bright, but what I've learned during my experience with younger men is that the part of their brain responsible for making decisions, *The Prefrontal Cortex* is not fully developed so they may not make the right choices. You said it yourself; this is a young man who is seriously in love with you. It is not about is career or even his first child. It's about love, something that you may never experience from a man ever again. You need to think this through because this might be your last chance to experience true love and having a family." "I guess your right Yvette, and I'm always willing to help him, he's so ambitious. I'm glad that I was able to open up and tell you." "I'm glad you did to, even though it was written all over your face." They relaxed on the couch, taking in the elements and Yvette showed Adriane additional photos of her and Jared. Two hours later, the guys returned barging in, with an up roar about who is now the better golfer. A chance of possible thunderstorms is broadcast, and Carmelo and Adriane decide to head back before getting soaked. They all promised to keep in touch and said a group prayer before making a swift exit.

# Chapter 14
# Wet Surface

*Simply Authentic*

L ow stratus clouds begin to form causing a dramatic change in the atmosphere. There are people scrambling for safety from the well-known hurricane winds, while Carmelo and Adriane sit patiently in the back seat of the cab. He totally forgot that Adriane was acting suspicious and said nothing about her behavior on their way to the hotel. The driver begins to get very irritable and begins shouting at the other cars and pedestrians on the street. Carmelo remains calm but the driver causes Adriane to begin feeling a little nauseous. She starts fidgeting and counting the seconds before she either explodes with anger or pukes all over Carmelo. They arrive back at the hotel as it now begins to pour. While exiting from the car, Carmelo wipes the tropical rain from her face before making their way to the elevator. Right after he opens the room door, she rushes into the bathroom. He's still unaware of their issue and enjoys the scenery by digging into his CD case and selects *"Summer Rain"* by Carl Thomas."

He removes his damped clothes and begins to unwind, while Adriane is in the bathroom puking her head off. It was well in the evening, but she was having morning sickness. While nearly bringing up a lung, she wondered whether if the omelets were fully cooked or maybe she drank the orange juice too fast, as well as a combination of both. She returned to the room only to see prince charming fast asleep near the window. The kiss that she applies to his forehead causes him to twirl in a more comfortable position. The conversation that she held with Yvette had replayed in her mind over and over again. She stares at Carmelo's boyish frame and began stroking his hairless chest. She then begins to clean out the microwave and selects a TV dinner. His favorite, the chicken parmesan with pasta, was quickly prepared as Carmelo was sure to have a huge appetite once he had awakened. She adds some pasta shells with cheese, lights some candles and cracked open the bottle of champagne that they received from the all guys table.

She showers and then wakes Carmelo by rubbing his forearm. He quickly showers and returns to the candle lit dinner with a huge smile on his face. Everything looked and smelled wonderful. After he says grace, they begin to recap on their individual time spent with Yvette and Jared. She refrains from spilling the beans as he guzzled his first glass, while sipping her half-filled glass. Carmelo began observing something different about her but thought that she was just tired and playfully suggested "Maybe I should have prepared our last dinner here together." She just replied with a smirk. Adriane was so exhausted that she couldn't even entertain the thought of Carmelo actually going into the kitchen and preparing a meal. She allowed him to eat a large portion of his dinner and watched him carefully as he swallowed completely, so that he would not choke once she gathered herself and nervously mentions "Carmelo I'm pregnant."

He sipped on the empty glass and then began wiping his

mouth without a napkin. He continues to wipe his mouth, while asking "Are you serious?" she confidently responds that she should be almost a month into her pregnancy. Carmelo continues his meal but the probing begins. "So if you're pregnant, why are you drinking?" "I haven't drank any of this; I only held the glass to my mouth." "O, I see, so you're playing mind games already." Adriane doesn't respond and he forgets that his glass is empty and attempts to take another sip. After a few seconds of silence, she refills his glass with a new bottle of wine. Carmelo is annoyed but assures his love for Adriane. He finishes the glass of wine within two sips and promises to support Adriane to the best of his ability. He takes a long look at her and pictures himself settling down and having a family. The news is shocking but Carmelo looks at this as a clean slate due to the many issues of raising his first born.

He repeats himself by guaranteeing that, he is dependable and once they return back to the states, his job hunt would begin immediately. He continues to thank her for creating such a beautiful setting to share such fantastic news. Adriane is more than convinced that Carmelo would do his very best and briefly considers having the baby. It's a gorgeous night and the mood is perfect. The storm has diminished to rain drops on the window sill and Carmelo has melted her heart with his marvelous lexis. She doesn't want to lead him on but there's no need to ruin their last night on vacation. So she decides to tell him that she has no plans on keeping the child once they return home. They finish dinner and lay in each other's arms until the sunrises. They both woke early the next morning and went for a walk and then had lunch at the beach restaurant. Carmelo ordered rum and pineapple juice alongside his fried dumplings and corn beef, while she had a virgin margarita and a fish platter. They toasted to a safe trip back home and took pictures standing on the beach.

Afterwards they went back to the hotel to finish packing and headed to the airport. It was exactly one hour before their flight and luckily they had no problem catching a cab, which got them to the airport in twenty minutes. Carmelo grabbed a snack right before they began boarding and took one last view of the luxurious sites. After being seated he struggles, but finally get his words together "I want thank you again beautiful for this magnificent trip, I had a wonderful time." "I had a great time as well, I really enjoyed myself. It was nice to finally leave the country for a while. I just wish that storm hadn't ruined our plans for Jamaica." "It's all good sweetie, I don't care what island I'm on as long as we're together. I'm just a little worried about how my mother is going to react once I tell her the news." Adriane attempts to take the load off Carmelo, by telling him to relax and reassures him that he has absolutely nothing to worry about. They arrive back in the city late that night and decide to go to Adriane's house as Dane was in Florida spending time with his father.

She calls Yvette to see if they returned home safely. Right after Yvette mentioned "Yes we're fine," she asked was her prediction correct once Carmelo received the news? "Yes you were right, he said that he would be there for me." Even though Carmelo was walking back and forth in the room Adriane still spoke in codes and informed Yvette that she wasn't going to tell Carmelo that she had plans to have an abortion until they got settled. "I couldn't bring myself to tell him last night because I didn't want to ruin our last night on vacation." "Are you sure you want to go through with this"? "Yes I'm sure, it's what's best for right now." "Ok, well I'll support you; take care of yourself until then. Maybe you guys could come to Chicago for a weekend."

Carmelo notifies his mother that they have arrived and would be home the next morning, but he mentions nothing about Adriane's pregnancy. Strangely, no questions are asked for why he didn't just come straight home? What's most important is that he had a great time and had returned safely. Adriane knows that Carmelo really misses his family and having him spend the night would certainly seem a little selfish. But Carmelo is a big boy, he grabs a glass of iced tea, kicks off his shoes and flicks through the channels. She knows that he is still feeling a bit shaky in keeping the news to himself, so having him spend the night is a good call. This would give her enough time to break the news to him, and then send him home to his mother in the morning. She carefully observes and notices that he is watching one of his favorite television shows. *"Two and a Half a men"*, which Carmelo strongly admired Charley Sheen. Adriane decides to take a shower and return at the end of the show. When she returned, Carmelo seemed to be dozing off, but this could not wait. The situation had become a strain on her conscious, even though she herself told Carmelo that he had nothing to worry about. She sits next to him and the vibe isn't good, he immediately asks "What, what's wrong?" "Carmelo I'm not planning on keeping the baby.

You have enough problems and I already have a mortgage." He begins to plea, "But I told you that I would be there for you, to help you and that's what I meant." He continued to press the issue until Adriane lashed out at him, "Carmelo you're broke, and even if you did get a job right now, you're still going to be broke, because now you would have two mouths to feed." "O, I get it now, it's all about the money" "No it's about reality, you need money in order to feed a child, you should already know that. I thought you would be glad that I'm doing you a favor by not screwing up your life." "Well, I just didn't see it that way. I actually thought maybe we could be a family, after the rough times passed." She kept her ground "Look I'm just not in a position to have a child at this point in my life. They're things that I would like to do with my life that doesn't include changing diapers at two am in the morning. You should also be aware of the fact that, a baby does not guarantee a couple staying together."

Carmelo had no choice but to remain silent after she ripped him a new one. That night he slept in the guest room, with

Adriane adding a little sarcasm. "You see this is working out perfectly, your already sleeping in the other room." The great Carmelo Johnson was completely drained and had no rebuttal. He didn't need the help of the, *Quiet Storm* radio show to help him relax, but he knew that Adriane was right. It was a candid moment in life, that he was being genuine and willing to do whatever it took to show this woman that he could step up to the plate and possibly show unbelievers, that this kind of relationship could work. Carmelo felt as though he was being cheated, similar to how a woman feels when she finds out that her significant other has been unfaithful. It was the first time they had ever gone to bed upset with each other. The next morning there was little said. But as usual breakfast was prepared, but no apologies were made.On the ride back to Carmelo's house, no date was discussed as to when she would be scheduling her procedure. He thought that she would change her mind, and just needed a little time to clear her head. In fact a little time was all she needed to make an appointment once she returned home. They arrive at his house and there's still a little tension between them, but Carmelo attempts to defuse it, by giving her a hug and kiss on the forehead. She pops open the trunk while his sister eagerly awaits him in the doorway. The princess remains anxious as he approaches with two suit cases and greets her with a big hug. His parents come outside and begin conversating with Adriane about how much fun they had. Adriane then gives an old fashion "O, look at the time, I should get going" and waves good bye to everyone after making a U-turn. Carmelo quickly unpacks his cloths and gives his parents the souvenirs that he bought for them.

The sea shells and a t- shirt were given to his little sister, while his parents loved the matching coffee mugs and key chains. His daughter was scheduled for a visit for the upcoming weekend, so he nicely wrapped her t-shirt and placed it inside a gift box along with a teddy bear until she arrived. Carmelo decides to take a nap, as everyone else makes a trip to the market for groceries. Anticipating a call from Adriane, he placed his cell phone right next to him on the bed and turns up the volume. His parents arrived a few hours later; more than likely, a trip was made to Grandpa Glenn's home to drop off a few items. While listening to my iPod, I got a text message from Carmelo mentioning that he had returned home earlier and was now getting ready to have dinner. Later that evening he showed his family photos of the gorgeous island as they took extreme liking to the ocean view from the hotel balcony. He later explained that they were not allowed to take pictures while visiting the historical sites.

His parents were happy that he got a taste of the Caribbean life style, and mentions that they really missed him. His father then mentioned that Jamaica has been doing quite well in the 2008 Olympic Games. Usain Bolt won the gold medal for the Men's 100m Finals, and Shelly-Ann Fraser won it for the women's team. Veronica Campbell-Brown won the gold medal for the women's 200m final. Jamaica also won the gold medal for the men's 4*100m Relay Final. Around nine o'clock that night I receive another text from Carmelo asking me to stop by. My family and I had just finished supper, so I jumped in my car and headed straight over to visit him. When I pulled in front of the house I could see the large bottle of Moscato, which gave me the clue that he was in need of venting. I welcomed him home as he poured me a glass of the cheap wine. "Adriane's Pregnant." I wasn't shocked that she was pregnant; I was more annoyed with his reaction of wanting her to keep the child. He was not thinking rationally. It certainly was not my place to suggest that Adriane should have an abortion, but as a friend, I had a personal and moral responsibility to advise him that he was condemning himself in this relationship. I praised him for mentioning that he would step up to the plate, and wanting to show her and others that he was more than just a fling, but having another child in the prime of his life would be foolish. I finally convinced him that if it was meant to be, then things would eventually work out whether or not she decides to have the baby. After his fifth glass of wine, he began to slur "Theo my good man, no woman, wife or concubine shall ever come between us." Once again Carmelo thanked me for being brutally honest and informed me how much our friendship meant to him. I then asked Carmelo, if he had spoken to her regarding her pregnancy since they had gotten back? He just mentioned that a little time to herself would be beneficial. I suggested that he give her a call just to check up on her but didn't have to discuss their dilemma.

He agreed, as I sipped on my third glass and sat on the steps. I can hear the phone ringing with Carmelo smiling and staggering back and forth. There's no answer but it was pretty late, so he just sent her a text message hoping that she sleeps well through the night. We continued to relax and even made a toast "To good blessings in the future." It's almost one o'clock in the morning and my wife has called me two million times. But Carmelo and I remain on his porch listening to the radio. About an hour later he receives a text message from Adriane mentioning that she's at Lankenau Hospital. He continues to scroll down, and the screen read "Something went wrong. "We immediately packed everything away, jumped in the car and went to the hospital. Adriane was admitted to the intensive care unit, where the doctor thought that we were her children, until Carmelo cogently corrected him and mentioned that he was her boyfriend. I sat outside the room returning my wife's messages as she threatens me with divorce for carousing. I simply assured her that I was assisting Carmelo with a crisis and to relax.

Dr. Jennings revealed that Adriane's blood pressure had fallen under the normal rate and she had a miscarriage. Carmelo had thanked me again for hanging out with him and strongly advised for me to return home to be with my family, unless I wanted to live in his parent's basement. While sitting by Adriane's bed side, she told Carmelo that after she left his home, she went to visit an old girlfriend that lived in Upper Darby. She began feeling dizzy but thought that she was just tired. She then began having stomach pains and that's when something obviously was going wrong. Typical Adriane wanted to be discrete and just told her girlfriend that she wanted to get back home in time to cook dinner for her son. She drove herself to the hospital and planned to texted Carmelo when she finally got a chance. Feeling vulnerable, she disclosed that she was uncertain whether to keep the baby. Despite making valid points that it was not in her best interest, she was in a deep stage of confusion and began crying as Carmelo wiped her tears. Seeing Adriane upset, didn't sit too well with Carmelo, so for the rest of the night he sat patiently by her bed side until she fell asleep.

# Chapter 15
# Maintaining

*The break down*

The next morning Dr. Jennings arrives with great news. Despite Adriane's low blood pressure her body had simply rejected the baby, and she was going to be released from the hospital. "I know it's not the best food Adriane but have some breakfast before leaving" the doctor suggested. He also suggested that she switch vitamins. The brand that she was currently taking often made her feel drowsy. Carmelo added that maybe a glass of wine would be suitable especially after a long day's work. The doctor agreed as he signed her discharge papers. Adriane gave Carmelo the car keys but she forgot where she parked. He hits the alarm button about four times and spots the vehicle in the B section of the parking lot. He just looks at her and shakes his head. She begins to snivel and says "I'm going straight home and back to bed." "Well I've heard that before, are you sure you're not going to run off to some secret hiding place?" "That would be nice, especially if you were coming with me, but no I'll be home resting, so call me later." Before leaving she thanks him with a kiss for coming to the hospital and remembers how lucky they both are to have each other.

Carmelo opens the door to his house and flops on the couch. He begins to stare at the beautiful picture of his daughter and becomes eager to spend some time with her. The upcoming weekend seems years away, but arrives in a flash. However he's swindled, and now finds it necessary to inform the authorities, but knows how aggravating the process can be. I recall drilling it into his head that "Nice guys finish last" as he continued to let these malicious actions transpire. Even though Adriane was aware of the issues pertaining to his daughter, Carmelo did his best never to burden her, or especially his beloved mother with all the drama. Both women often advised him to temporarily remove himself from his daughter's life, and allow time to heal the wounds. But a very determined Carmelo had the nerve to pursue being in his daughter's life. This young black man actually had the audacity to continue going up to her school, to pick her up and spend an enormous amount of money on his little world.

Several months had passed and Carmelo's unemployment benefits were depleting. He was uncertain of a possible extension and began applying for every customer service position on earth. His next scheduled weekend arrives, and he plans another great day with the princess. She has an early dismissal from school, and he's sure to be on time. Alissa is thrilled to see her father and jumps in his arms upon his arrival. He called home a few times but there was no answer, so they hurry to check on his mother, before heading out to have some lunch and maybe picking up a few items. Mrs. Andrews is fine, but shockingly Carmelo gets into an altercation. The day is ruined but he still proceeds in purchasing a number of outfits for the princess. He informed Adriane about the confrontation, which she urged for him to back off until the baby is older, because it's clear that she is being manipulated. He and I met up later on that night, at a pool hall in old city, where I congratulated him for not retaliating. After a few drinks we both concluded that he's a genius due to his cool demeanor, during all of the hate and dreadful actions that were being thrown at him. A few days had passed and everything seemed to be normal. He even landed a position with a security company in center city. The immaculate thirty floor building catered to a number of different organizations and law offices. It surely wasn't his line of work but it would help his parents with the bills.

Right after the interview he wanted to celebrate the good news with Adriane, but she was already out the door and heading to work. Three other nurses decided to call out sick the same night of the *"New Kids on the Block"* reunion concert. He was due to start his new job the next day. Grandpa Glenn even gave him a couple of ties to wear with his all black uniform, which gave Carmelo the look of a secret service agent. Unfortunately this so called victim made a complaint against Carmelo on the day he picked up his daughter and a warrant was issued for his arrest. He was taken into custody around five thirty in the morning, and missed work. Carmelo had been working so hard to find a job to support his family and to establish his relationship with Adriane, in the error that many had considered a depression, and now this huge set back was obviously intended to destroy his progress. It kept getting worse, during his hearing Carmelo lost his temper and offered the judge a few choice words, he was held in contempt, bail was denied and with a court date scheduled a few months away. Everyone was devastated; he kept great communication with me and his mother, but seldom called Adriane. He would go weeks without calling her. Dealing with a woman's emotions and questioning her loyalty was irrelevant, as he had to adjust his mind frame to "Nothing, or no one on the outside matters."

When he did speak with her, their conversations would be brief and Carmelo never questioned her about seeing other men.

He spent most of his time in the law library and enhancing his physical appearance. A philosophical approach was implemented, as it was a time to reposition himself and continue on a positive journey, once he was released. His cell mate, Darren James who had an unfortunate run in with the police, and who worked in the law library kept Carmelo's mind stimulated on how the court system is corrupt and in some cases intentionally rail road's the future of young black men. Darren was only twenty three years of age and extremely courageous. He assured Carmelo that victory would be the outcome of his trial because, no jury or judge in his correct state of mind would find him guilty of the bizarre allegations. "This was a slam dunk case." Carmelo decided that bettering his relationship with God wasn't a bad idea, since it was obviously a lesson to be learned from this disaster.

He wasn't too crazy about receiving a visit from either of us but he couldn't help but to think about Adriane, he missed her dearly. At night her chocolate complexion vigorously appeared in his pitch black cell. Whenever he applied his coco butter, he could still feel her skin because they were one. After four months of being incarcerated Carmelo's big day in court had finally arrived. Even with graduating from college, having a promising career, and being a positive role model in his daughter's life. Carmelo was not spared the sword of exploitation. He was found guilty for two counts of simple assault, endangering the welfare of a child and condemned to ten years' probation. His private attorney appealed the tyrant's decision in less than a week. He was sentenced to an additional thirty days and remained extremely confident that things would turn out in his favor. His countdown began to being discharged from what was actually one of the best universities he's ever attended. He was transferred to a different section of the facility after his trial, but kept close ties with Darren. His new cell mate Khenti, migrated from Egypt and had been incarcerated for several months for an altercation that occurred at one of Carmelo's favorite restaurants.

As a devoted Jehovah's Witness, Khenti also spoke several different languages. He was a huge inspiration by teaching Carmelo a few French terms, which would only make him more impressive with the ladies. Unfortunately Carmelo's lessons were cut short due to his name being called for a discharge two weeks before his twenty seventh birthday. He quickly packed his things, said a quick prayer with Khenti and flew out of there, like a bat out of hell. He was given one token and seventy five cents for a transfer, and released exactly one thirty in the morning. Carmelo ran down the dark streets jumping over trash cans and hopped on the first bus that he saw. He was unsure of the destination, but it was just his luck that the bus was going in his direction, which was the Frankford terminal. The car fare was not enough to get him straight home, so he decided to spend the night at his grandfather's home. Grandpa Glenn kept an old fashion conduct of keeping his door unlocked, so Carmelo crept up the stairs and into his room. Struggling to open his eyes, Grandpa Glenn took a few seconds to realize that his grandson had returned home. They embraced each other and Carmelo mentioned that he would be spending the night and then going home in the morning. He slept peacefully for the remainder of the night and arised several hours later to raid the fridge. Right before Carmelo's Step- father arrived to take him home, he stood on the porch taking in the fresh air. Everything seems much different but he just continues to grasp on to the feeling of freedom.

Grandpa Glenn begins to spew words of encouragement before he's rushed by his step-father. "Let's get going, your mother will be waiting for you back at the house." On their way back Carmelo constantly makes eye contact with several women waiting for the bus. The sixty five flies past and he pictures himself heading back into the city to enroll in school and trying to get his job back. He thanks his father again for the ride, and runs upstairs where his mother is resting. He almost knocked the door off the hinges and gave his mother a huge bear hug. After a thousand kisses he demands the left overs from Sunday dinner. He takes a long hot shower and then explains his plans at the dinner table, which includes picking up where he left off with school and work, but removing himself from his daughter's life would be necessary. He apologizes for not taking his mother's advice and painfully removing himself sooner. Experience is the best teacher and his parents are just delighted that the heir to their throne has returned home safely. His mother compliments him on his new chiseled frame, while he request for seconds. His little sister is still in school and Carmelo plans on surprising her with an early dismissal but a stat nine exam is in progress and ruins his plans. He returns to his room and gets comfortable to make his first phone call to Adriane. It's about four thirty and she should be home by now. Her phone rings three times but there's no answer. He just left a message letting her know that he had made it back home in one piece and suggested that she stop by if she was still on the road. It didn't take long for his mother's home cooking to settle in, as he quickly fell asleep. In less than one hour, the phone rings and Adriane's name appears on the screen. He clears his voice and assumed that she was on her way to see him. "Hey beautiful, Are you on your way over?" "No, sorry Carmelo I'm not going to be able to make it over there, I'm really tired." Carmelo knew Adriane like the back of his hand. He just served a total of five months in prison and her excuse for not being able to see him, was because she was tired.

The deceit in her tone causes his hand to tremble, and he can't swallow due to the dryness in his throat. He assumes that waiting one more day to see her wouldn't hurt, since it's been this long, but that's until she drops the atomic bomb on him. "Carmelo I'm going to tell you that things are going to be different" his heart begins to race and he steps inside his walk in closet in fear of him raising his voice. "What do you mean?" while clearing his throat.

She replies "Things are not going to be like they use to be." He repeats "What do you mean, have you been seeing someone else?" "Yes Carmelo I have," "Is it Dane's father?" "No, it's not but he has been trying to rekindle things between us for a long time." Then Carmelo asks the magic question "Well did you sleep with him." She refuses from answering the question, which Carmelo is now filled with rage, but here comes the dagger, "Come on Carmelo, you know that this had to end. Were we really going to have a fairy tale? Maybe this was how it was supposed to end."

He doesn't want to disrespect his parent's home but Carmelo is seconds away from releasing a hail of obscenities. He also knows that Adriane would hang up the phone, which would cause him to be more irate. A brief moment of silence is needed to gather his thoughts and Carmelo is stung by the humble bug and puts the entire ordeal in perspective. "Thank you, thank you Adriane for all that you have done for me. We had a tremendous run. I just didn't want to continue being a burden, that's why I stopped calling you. If I would have listened to you and my mother, and just stepped away, I would have never been in that predicament. But I'm glad that I fought for my daughter. I'm glad that I never accepted the offer from an old friend to move to Arizona, even before I met you. All the custody hearings, the swindling by the courts, my brief prison stay, the child support payments being thrown back in my face, the police station arrangements, the supervised visits at the court house, picking up the child early, or not sending her to school on the days that I was scheduled to have her, and the phony allegations to the Department of Human Services for child abuse. I'm eternally grateful to experience such adversity.

I'm glad that I stayed and established that bond that can never be broken between a father and his daughter. She and I had some great times, and I have all the pictures to remind her and the court documents that were filed on my behalf that I fought for her. So the drama was all worth it." "Your right, and to be honest, I don't know if I would have walked away that easy if Dane's father was giving me all that drama." "But it's alright Adriane, you deserve to be happy. You were good to me and I am extremely lucky that you gave me the time of day." Adriane agreed that the relationship surely lasted longer than either of them ever imagined. It was sad to see how it ended, due to Carmelo being incarcerated for foolishness. His character and imprisonment was like the greatest blasphemy of all mankind but continued to expose the modern day, *Jim Crow Laws*. Adriane guaranteed a friendship and told him that he could still call her if he needed anything, and that she hoped the feeling was mutual. After the hour conversation they hung up wishing the best for each other. Carmelo's speech was sincere but deep down he still held a little resentment towards Adriane. But it didn't take long for him to realize that, if they were to switch places during those five months, he would have been intimate with someone else.

Hours pass and he hears a soft knock at the door. He opens it, and his little sister is standing there with a huge smile on her face and jumps into his arms. She asks about her niece, which he replies that she's doing just fine, and begins tickling her. Another hug is given to the princess and she runs off to take a nap. Of course he had a stack of mail and over two thousands e-mails to review, but before cleaning his inbox that evening, he and I went out for Long Island Iced Teas and Buffalo wings. He had been home less than a week and was invited to a photo shoot for a modeling agency in New York. He bought a twenty dollar round trip ticket, but unfortunately it turned out to be a sham. The agency was requesting a four hundred dollar fee to get started, and Carmelo remembered the golden rule, which was "Never to pay any money." If a company is really interested in you, they should be offering you a check." The trip wasn't a complete waste as he enjoyed the, *Big Apple* but returned home in time to get his job back the following week.

He refused to spend the remaining of his twenties going through unnecessary circumstances. More than likely he couldn't erase certain people out of his life; he was just eager to begin a new one. When purchasing his new cell phone he switched carriers and changed the number. He didn't feel that it was necessary to give Adriane his new number, or to have her as a contact. Carmelo remembered how jealous he felt when one of her old boyfriend's occasionally would call just to check up on her. He respected his fellow male species differently, and held them in high standards, regardless if Adriane gave him permission to continue calling her. His twenty seventh birthday passed with no phone call from her. Even though she didn't have his new number, she could have still called the house number, which she did quite often when he didn't answer his cell phone. Carmelo established himself back on the social scene but thoughts of Adriane would appear whenever he was intimate with other women. At times he thought about calling her back and giving her a piece of his mind, but that would only have tarnished his rendition of ending things with class. He thought about donating the expensive fleece robe that she bought for him the previous year to the Red Cross, but changed his mind. *It was that nice.* The feeling was weird when leaving the library and not having her waiting for him, making her sly college boy remarks.

At times Carmelo would drift into a rage of jealousy wondering what this new boyfriend of hers looked like. However, he never exposed himself, in this manner of immature curiosity and give Adriane the confirmation that she had done well by moving on. Usually lonely nights would hinder someone's progress when coping with a bad break up, but for Carmelo many nights were spent enjoying the inspirational cool sounds of Maxwell and Robin Thicke. His egotistical mind frame was surely a big help by depicting that this new guy had to be financially stabled and was not better looking than him. It couldn't have been the sex because everything was great in that department. Now that Carmelo had returned home, she's sticking with her possibly well-off replacement. When Thanksgiving arrived Carmelo went to his Grandfather's home and received a message from his mother that she called. It's like a woman wanting an expensive dress and once she receives it, the feeling is more casual instead of classy. Carmelo is supposed to be excited, or at least feels the need to return her call, but he doesn't. He responds to his mother with a head nod and a simple "ok", while switching the channel. What a year Brett Favre is having in his first season as a Minnesota Viking, with an amazing run to the Super Bowl. However during guy's night out we tried to make sense of Adriane's decision making. Carmelo was a square guy, so if it wasn't because of financial assurance, then why wouldn't she continue a relationship with Carmelo? It was happy hour at a new tavern in center city and Sean and I scarfed down a large portion of crab fries, while Carmelo and Eden craved a chicken cheese steak and beer. Sean noted that some people change along with their circumstances.

Which led Carmelo to asked "So why should Adriane be exempt from the, *Gold Digger* label?" I agreed with him and stated that "Maybe she was looking for someone that was financially stabled. I'm confident that if you were rich, she would have kept the baby and gone out of her way to communicate with you, like with a simple letter. It would not have been about how much she wanted to do with her career. Her new occupation would have been in collections, because collecting a check would be her new career. So I'm not buying that it's about my career bull rap." "Very true, and also comical", Carmelo stated. Eden simply confirmed that "You just had an unfortunate vacation. When Eden stated the obvious, it gave Carmelo the chance to elaborate and we were all ears. A double shot of Jack Daniels caused him to unleash, "So where is the loyalty on her behalf, on any woman's behalf when their significant other is temporarily removed from society? You see! Adriane invested a little, just in case I was to get rich and famous. Then she would be there to reap all the benefits. But unfortunately during the ride to a secured life style, she abandoned ship and forfeits her treasure." I agreed with him because he made a valid point about her investing, Carmelo was prince charming but was struggling financially. And towards the end of their relationship Adriane paid for the majority of their dinners and hotel stays. However Sean and Eden were not convinced. We ended the night with shots of Hennessey, and planned on meeting up a few days later.

# Chapter 16
# Reassessment

*Shock Value of Tradition*

H is story and strange encounters are certainly classical, like the time he became well acquainted with a bike patrol officer by the name of Jamison. Both men had cordial conversations in passing, with Jamison providing words of encouragement for Carmelo to remain a positive young man and to complete his education. Jamison was also well aware of Carmelo's preference in women and provided a token of wisdom. "Some of the older women are crazier and have more issues than some younger women. It's due to economic stressors and them being screwed over by their fathers or during relationships." Weeks later, after running a few errands, Carmelo took interest in a mid-age-woman that was waiting for her bus at the sixty ninth street terminal. He's had numerous success interrupting a woman's conversation while she spoke on the phone but this time, it would be a complete disaster.

After rejecting Carmelo, he simply replied to the woman that she should be more polite when receiving a compliment. That comment didn't sit too well with her as she lashed out at him and caused a scene, he sat calmly with his legs crossed and a huge smile on his face. He decides to entertain this absurd person as she continues to make a spectacle of herself and simply over reacting to his charm. "You're an extremely bitter and angry woman." He repeats it several times in a row which only irritates the wretch. It gets better, after a few minutes of silence, Jamison appears in plain clothes; it's safe to assume he had just finished working his shift. He greets Carmelo with a handshake and walks over to the woman. It's his wife, and within seconds the woman erupts again. Jamison stands shocked and speechless, while Carmelo is in disbelief, but remains calm on the bench with his legs crossed. She begins to exaggerate, while both men glance at each other. Carmelo reflects on Jamison's token of wisdom and begins to process how the officer might have acquired first-hand experience dealing with women that had a mental disturbance. Nevertheless, Carmelo ended the feud with an apology and handshake with Jamison. The coincidence was no hinder to their association as both men were able to find humor in the awkward moment as they routinely crossed paths.

Carmelo learned that some older women tend to be one dimensional and was stuck in their ways. Their accustomed to tradition, which prevents them from adapting to this stage of socializing with a younger audience. This belief was confirmed after he briefly conversed with Ms. Robin Tillery. They met in Center City during the last days of the Christmas rush. She was a remarkable stock investor with three children. Robin had no intentions of calling Carmelo until she was persuaded by a close friend who was dating a younger man. She admitted that Carmelo was a very intriguing young man, but she failed to convert to the well accepted trend. While pursuing another beauty, he was instantly rejected, but recalled the Julianna Margulies look alike mentioning that "It's nothing new for older women to date younger men; it was just well hidden by some participators."

Carmelo often praised the creators of *Flirting with Forty*, *Cougar Town* and the reality show *"The Cougar."* These shows were generally created for entertainment, but they inspired woman who continued to believe that being in a relationship with a man, perhaps twenty years younger would never work. Carmelo also recalled Robin mentioning that "I doubt if anything serious would have occurred, because you're so young." Those were also the same exact words of Belinda during a debate and he was clever, "Compatibility is not certain with someone because you're both in the same age bracket. Your chances of making a love connection increases when you allow yourself to explore all paths which lead to possibilities. Have you taken a look at the divorce rate in America lately? Never mind the break up rate for those who are just causally dating." He was passionate about inspiring women over the age of forty to have this inclination and his views were extraordinary, "It's nothing short of pure madness not to try something new because of how you were brought up, or the very worst, what someone else said or may have experienced.

What's more effective when establishing a successful relationship between two different generations? Is it what you've been taught or your own personal experience? You can read any novel, watch any television show, and attend as many sermons throughout the year, but your own personal experience will be the best teacher." It wasn't until college that Carmelo learned the exact definition for insanity, which consists of repeating the same actions and expecting different results. "That's exactly what happens when some women continue their ancient way of life. Their stubbornness and lack of ability will only lead to pure bitterness and resentment to those who adapt and find the courage to re- evaluate their thought process. The haters will re-live their second childhood and begin calling you names and passing negative remarks behind your back, such as you must be desperate, and you should be ashamed of yourself. Only a few will be bold enough to ask, why can't you find someone your own age? Do you think it's really going to work? Their questions might seem valid, but their intentions are to discourage you. What if he wants children? What would his parents think? Or more importantly, what would your children think? You can't be serious. Remember that its pure jealousy and they would love to have your position, which is simply to be happy.

Regardless if it's only for the moment, that's one more day that you laughed, and had electrifying sex. That's one more day that your colleagues mentioned that you were glowing, instead of being stuck in a sardine can, displeasing relationship." Carmelo was often told that he was like a breath of fresh air and made women feel free. He enjoyed those compliments that confirmed he was doing something right. He stressed that "Women who refused to break out of their shell are limiting themselves to finding true happiness. Trying to establish a relationship with someone that is young enough to be your child, is no different than establishing one with someone your own age. Assuming that this young man is legal, you would generally ask the same questions. Are you employed? Would you like to be married, in the near future? Would you like to have children? Would you like anymore, if either of you already children?

But what's more important is, ask yourself these same questions because you might not want any of these things. Marriage may not be in your future, you might be finish with having children, so what difference does it make about the persons age? As long as your happy and having a great time. Other people's opinion is irrelevant, because you're content. There's certainly less stress due to the non-obligation to one another if that's the arrangement. Don't kill yourself with the relentless interrogation, but more frequently asked questions are "Well what happens in twenty years when I'm sixty or seventy and no longer have the physical appearance of a younger woman? What if I fall terminally ill? What are the chances with him being a younger man want to handle the demanding obligations of assisting with my basic needs? Ask yourself what condition your health will be in for the next twenty years. Focus on what's more important like not smoking, not drinking too much, watching your weight, exercising, getting your mammograms, and simply putting yourself in the position to be around to see the next twenty years. You may be in your fifties and have flirted with the idea to have another child. Well the possibilities of that happening surely will decrease if you choose to pay less attention to the previous factors."

Furthermore, the average age of women becoming mothers has risen in the United States, and in the last twenty years, a few women have even entered motherhood in their sixties. By implanting embryos produced by in-vitro fertilization using egg cells donated by younger women, women who have passed menopause can become pregnant and give birth. In February of 2012, a study of one hundred and one women age fifty and older who had children using donated eggs revealed that pregnancy at this age carries about the same risk as similarly induced pregnancies in younger women. The study is the largest one to date looking at pregnancy in post-menopausal women. "These women do pretty well, "said Dr. Sauer, senior author of the article and chief of the division of reproductive endocrinology and infertility at Columbia University Medical Center, where all the women in the study received IVF.

"If they're well-screened and well cared for, they really should do O.K., "Sauer said. "These are smart, educated, well-off women that are doing this, "he said, and pregnancy after fifty is not common-the one hundred one cases in the study were collected over a decade. So with that information Carmelo seems to be on the right track as far as your health is concerned. But he continued to have the floor, "Wouldn't it make more sense if your husband is a younger man, just in case you become terminally ill?" "Wouldn't it benefit the woman to have someone that was in better standards of health?" "Having someone that could run around, back and forth to the hospital, instead of lying next to you in the emergency room just seems more logical." Carmelo joked that "At the very least I could do is get a nurse for her ass", but for the less fortunate, family support and a deceit insurance plan from her employer should suffice." After we paced around his neighborhood, he elaborated, "If women are concerned about their physical appearance when entering the senior citizen stage, again this can easily be resolved. "He just looked at me and smiled, while pointing across the street at the beautiful goddess jogging towards us. Golden boy is well aware that one of the cardinal rules is to never ask a woman her age, but he disregards the basic principle. She removes her headphones and takes liking to his charming demeanor and confidently replies that she's sixty six. Although happily married for forty years, Ms. Anita confirmed Carmelo's views and proved a great grandmother could still be very attractive. Feel free to strut around town with your new companion. As you could see, Adriane and her young messiah reached a level of comfort and even attended church services together. At first, you might feel uncomfortable like Larraine, or you might fall head over heels like Belinda and become obsessed. All relationships has its stages of developments. Even a one night stand has to develop an extreme amount of chemistry, unless the woman is actually that permissive. Carmelo intends, for woman around the world to have a new perspective on life. Provide that college boy, or that hot landscaper the opportunity to bless you with the same love, affection and commitment, which every woman deserves to experience.

By now, you may be wondering, well where the hell is he? Do I have to go to the local college or club? Honestly, you could!

But the library, and the museums are pretty good places to meet young intelligent guys with a bright future. Church is definitely an option. *What a great place to actually meet your husband if you're seeking a good, strong wholesome man!* The last place that you would want to meet a guy is a club. You can't even hold a decent conversation in that type of environment. Carmelo's remains taking additional courses at community college and was recently informed by one of his perspective choices that upon transferring, he would more than likely complete undergrad within a year. His appeal was granted and his case was dismissed.

He remains one of the most eligible bachelors and hopes that new cougar chasers will emerge and join him on the prow in making older women a top priority when searching for true love. There are thousands, perhaps millions of guys out there that would love to date an older woman but simply lack the confidence to introduce themselves. These are the same guys that would approach every young lady in the city, but when an older, more dominant woman steps on the scene, the guys are intimidated and have a fear of rejection.

Carmelo suggested that, implementing the fact that you will be denied at least half the time because of reasons that were previously mentioned in this chapter, and also women that are in their forties are usually already married. However, establishing your independence would be the first priority. Convenience is better than having the luxury of a nice car. Some younger men often make the error of placing their focus on receiving the attention and not realizing that women love to spend quality time. Having a nice car is great, and both generations of women will submit their desires in the alternative. But a real woman will have more respect for you, if your independence is established. It was a necessity that Carmelo lacked for the most part, but was fortunate to still be successful. As he matured, Carmelo's wardrobe began to evolve, which complimented his excellent mannerism. "You're only allowed one first impression, so why not introduce yourself as a grown and sexy, well dressed young man?"

He advised that your style must be unique. If it applies, you'll simply replace your outdated jeans, with a pair of nice fitted khakis. The sweat shirts are moved to the bottom of the dresser and replaced with, V-neck, cashmere sweaters. Make an affordable selection of any casual blazers, platoon and wool pea coats that will replace those old winter jackets. Learn a woman's way of re- evaluating her life style and treat yourself to entire makeover. Don't allow some authors who write these self-help books, to persuade you that you're only changing your appearance, not who you are. Unfortunately in today's society, you are judged by your appearance. You are the best person to represent yourself. You're not changing your entire life style, just certain attributes that will make you more appealing to women. You often hear the popular concept that "The way to a man's heart is through is stomach", well that also applies to women. Nice jewelry, and cars are the main attractions, however both generations of women love a man that is capable of preparing a well cooked meal and then sexing them crazy.

Elevate your mind in being accustomed to reading certain books that will extend your vocabulary. This is the most essential method in connecting with women. Both generations of women love to have long great conversations. Remember that Carmelo was able to captivate Belinda during their five hour discussions over the phone, which led to him being invited to her home a few weeks later. Even by watching certain television shows, you're connecting with women. You're establishing a level of having similar interest. Talk shows are certainly a great topic of discussion, along with the long list of crime investigations shows that air during the week. A sophisticated woman is only going to have a conversation that contains substance. More than likely their dialogues would concern universal health care, religion, bettering the environment and nice places to relax on the weekends. Establishing your credit, purchasing a home and having a family are more advance discussions if you're granted an opportunity to convey one.

Unlike their younger counter parts who are easily manipulated into sleeping with you after a movie and going to a chain restaurant, you must also know how to have fun with an older woman. Older women usually don't tolerate a lot of noise, where you're forced to raise your voice at the dinner table. Choose a restaurant that is classy but still affordable, and that will provide you with the convenience and courtesy. This will minimize the typical loud and obnoxious crowd being rude to the servers. Both generations of women would love to enjoy a beautiful outing. But choosing a secluded restaurant would be more suitable for an older woman, especially at the beginning of the relationship. This setting would surely put her at ease, just in case she feels uncomfortable when looking at you and seeing her son. Carmelo chose his words carefully and was extremely comical, which earned him extra points with both generations. He's not recommending for you to become a comedian the entire night, but take it easy and the jokes will come naturally.

Continue the ancient gestures such as helping with her coat and pulling out her chair. It doesn't have to be a holiday for you to brighten her day with roses. When Carmelo got his job back, he pleasantly surprised the Vice President for the YMCA, by having flowers delivered to her office. Unfortunately she was involved but he continues to set the standards of how women should be treated. Confirmation was epic when dating older women and was simply himself. "Older women have a broad range of experience and they have heard it all, seen it all, some have even done it all. They already know what's going to come out of your mouth, and assume that by being a younger guy, you're going to say something that's a complete turn off. However assumptions are good and can work in your favor; it gives you the chance to surprise them, especially when you initiate discussions of their favorite topics as previously mentioned. Understand that it is critical for women to acknowledge that you are unique, and do not conduct yourself like the average twenty year old. These are the fundamentals of connecting with an older woman. Carmelo's assessments of dating were exceptional, but what was more fascinating, was when he elaborated on the similar behavior and emotions of women from both age groups.

"Both generations have a tendency to whine and try to prove themselves, in any discussion." During all three of Carmelo's experiences he was often tormented when they failed to have his undivided attention. All three women irritated him by leaving threatening messages to end the relationship and portrayed the same behavior of younger immature females. Instead of going to small claims court, like the contract mentioned, Larraine decides to inform her boyfriend of the issue. The typical younger woman might find humor by mentioning that she is pregnant. That is the absolute worse joke to play on a young man, or any man that's ambitious. Adriane often annoyed Carmelo by mentioning that "Little C J, was on the way", until it became true. Both generations of women even share the same infatuations which are shopping for jewelry and clothes. Statistic show that fifty percent of marriages end in divorce, with the main reason being financial difficulty and debt. After having dozens of experiences with women over the age of forty. Carmelo's views were profound and changed his tactic on dating. It might be a little off topic, but is extremely relevant when establishing a relationship. During numerous debates on relationships he annihilated his female opponents. "Some older women or perhaps women in general are less aggressive and fearful of approaching and introducing themselves to a guy. If they continue with this traditional mind frame of a man making the first move, they will continue to poison their offspring.

You may be guilty of making these comments, or often hear women state that "If a man doesn't approach me first, then it's not meant to be", "I would never approach a man." These types of women are all cut from the same defects that create basic colors of a relationship that will eventually fade. This concept actually puts a strain on a good man because he could be a shy person, or possibly not even have noticed you. If women expect men to approach them with confidence and respect, why not extend the same courtesy? R&B giants, Beyonce and Ciara have made songs boasting about having tendencies, if they could act like a boy, due to the negative things that guys do in relationships. Well building up the courage to approach a beautiful woman and taking the chance of being embarrassed is one of the risks that we take every day. Women have established an enormous amount of financial independence. Controversial topics still surface today about the roles being reversed, where some husbands stay at home and the wife is the bread winner and provides financially for the family. Women now are even running for President, ok fine, that's great! So if there's so many independent women out there, what's wrong with a woman consistently picking up the tab on the first, second or even third date? It's safe to assume that you can tell if a guy is taking advantage of you, so why not consider making the initial contact?" Carmelo is not bashing women, but these are valid questions.

# Chapter 17
# Go get her

*Last Call...*

I t's the spring of 2009, and several months after his release. Carmelo took some time off from school but is working two jobs and is doing quite well. He landed a second position on the weekends working in Manayunk, as a concierge for a luxurious loft facility. After getting a quick glimpse of the other two candidates, who decided to be casual and tacky, Carmelo figured that he really didn't have too say much, accept sit and wait for a phone call, which came a few days after the interview. He observes his new boss and Property Manager, Marissa Blair who is petite, mid-age, and attractive with dark colored hair in a ponytail. She begins rambling, after informing him of the minute job description of basically, staying well groomed, sitting at a desk from eight pm to eight o'clock the next morning, and making small talk with the tenants during that time. She's also borderline flirtatious after complementing him on his suit. It's the perfect pretty boy job for Carmelo, as his colorful shirts and pocket squares easily drew attention. One dashing, young marketing rep encouraged him to, "Continue dressing for the job you want, not for the job you have." But Carmelo enjoyed working at the lofts. It was a wonderful addition to his first part time job, which was three days a week, three to eleven o'clock at night. It also would increase his funds after using his income tax to pay for six months of rent in advance for his new bachelors pad.

The charming one bed room was close to his parents and didn't require working overtime to make the payments. He even managed to befriend a tenant that was the brother of the 76ers who gave him, a brand new all black leather living room set for free. Fortunately for myself and the rest of the guys, he currently doesn't have a love interest and reserves every Friday night for guy's night out. He's had a number of experiences but nothing substantial. It's nearly a year since Adriane, but when coincidence appears he's constantly reminded of their endeavors. Center city was a torture chamber, their favorite hotels and restaurants were constantly filled with intoxicated romancers and spectators in search of love.

He would stroll pass the numerous designer stores and get a whiff of her Chanel perfume. A new restaurant had just opened and displayed a sample menu in the window, which they offered her favorite appetizer, the broccoli cheese soup. He had never gone to visit Adriane by himself the entire time they dated, and scarcely recalls the directions she gave him. Of course it would be insane to suddenly pop up at her door after so long, while contemplating she must have accomplished her dreams, and at the very least was engaged by now. Destroying his old phone and not saving her as a contact surely wasn't a great idea. But there was no time for wishful thinking, and create falsehood. Adriane still had his heart and he needed a plan. We first decided, to give the city a break and select one of the pubs on Main Street, in Manayunk. Sean's first suggested that he takes the lead role of becoming Magnum

PI, while Eden simply mentioned retracting his old phone bills and do a prank call from an anonymous number to see if she answers. Carmelo suggested implementing that idea with his former employer, Dons. If she is there, he would send a half dozen of pink roses, which were her favorite, along with his new number. The plan would have been more simple and less thrilling, if I was scheduled to work that day, and just told Carmelo whether or not she was there. We kept Sean's hilarious plan in reserve just in case Carmelo failed.

I remind Carmelo that it's an excellent plan, and also of the illegal dilemma of stalking. "It's not stalking, funny guy, because I'm revealing myself with the flowers." Its early Monday morning, he just completed a sixteen hour shift, but he's filled up with octane. After heading home to drop off his satchel, he changes, and jogs to City Avenue where he makes the anonymous call from a gas station. A new secretary answers and transfers him to the nurse's station. Unexpectedly, Adriane picks up; he really never recognized her voice and proceeded in disguising his. "Who is this?" She asked while being highly suspicious, but certainly wouldn't expect that Carmelo would play such childish games so early in the morning. He began coughing like a sicko and hung up the phone. Ok great, she answered the phone around nine o'clock, which meant that she would be there until three. That also would give the florist enough time to get there. He placed the order and was assured that the delivery would be there in a matter of hours. He only hopes that, Adriane does not leave before then or worse, she gets the flowers and throws them in the trash in fear of her lover seeing them. He then jogs back home and gets a few hours of rest until it's time for work at three o'clock.

A few hours later, he awakes with a missed call from a number he doesn't recognize. There's a voice mail message that he anxiously checks, but it's a representative from a collections agency requesting a payment for a student loan. It's now two thirty, and before walking into work he received another voice male notification. He never received the call due to having no underground service. He has small talk with the, YMCA vice president and makes his way to the bathroom to check the message. Finally, it's Adriane thanking him for the flowers and that they were right on time, because she was having a long day. She leaves her number and informs him to call whenever he has a chance. He texted Sean, informing him that his services would not be needed and after getting settled and watching his boss slowly walk out the door, his highly anticipated call is made. She answers right before he was going to hang up, and thanks him again for the gesture. "Those roses smelled so good, everyone was soo jealous, especially my supervisor, whose marriage is on the rocks." Without hesitation, "Speaking of the rocks, how about a drink?" "Wow, you're really on point today, aren't you? I could also use one of those, where are you? "I'm at work down town, nineteen hundred JFK Boulevard, and I usually take a two or three hour lunch break. It's only me and my colleague Stanford here in the building, and we have a pretty good buddy system going. Is six o'clock ok?" "That's perfect; I'm actually pulling up in front of my house as we speak. Wow this is scary, but I can't wait to see you, it's been a while." "Likewise."

Failure wasn't expected of him, but I was absolutely shocked when he informed me that she was basically on her way to see him. Uncharacteristically, he began to question his own luck. "Maybe she's still with that other guy and things aren't going so well and just wants to hang out." But I remind him that "Adriane isn't that type of woman, she would have simply ended the relationship. She's too old for that", as she just recently celebrated her forty seventh birthday." He playfully fires back, and protects the rekindling flame, "Choose your words carefully young smith, you meant to say that she's too mature. Insult her again and I'll have you beheaded before night fall." "My apologies, Lord

Johnson, but I thought you said, no wife or concubine would come between us." "That's correct, but I didn't say Goddess." Such humor! I needed a good laugh as my kids were driving me nuts. It's now just about that time but Adriane arrives about ten minutes late, which is not bad for the week day traffic. My comrade was looking sharp, with his hair brushed about thirty times, a quick spit shine for his shoes, and an extra dash of Acqua di Gio cologne applied to his new Jos. A. Bank suit, giving him the appearance of a young executive.

With a nineteen year age difference, there's no need for a watch, he's well aware that this is his time. She steps out of her car with the same gleaming smile, and removes her sun glasses to get a better look at his advanced stature, and a light wind passes exposing her sexy cerise color panties. Her matching all-purpose dress and shoes blends perfectly with her completion. Still being embarrassed, she greets him with a long hug, while hiding her face in his chest. He then takes a deep breath and is amazed at her youthfulness, before showing her off to his elderly co-worker, who almost loses his dentures while shaking her hand. He gives Carmelo the thumbs up as they head back out into the evening breeze. Adriane's much careful this time and wholes her dress, as Carmelo gives directions to the exquisite back entrance of the Four Season's Hotel. They crossed a small bridge with night lights, which lead the diners pass a stone mountain waterfall. They seat themselves and she's taken by the romantic scenery, and tranquility of the secluded area. Even better, they have complete privacy when their order of wine arrives. Adriane thanks him with "A toast to great health, and remaining incredibly handsome." He's not drunk, but foolishly replies, "Your welcome, I'm glad I called." "What, what do you mean? I never got a call from you." He tried to interrupt and change the subject but failed. "No, no, no wait a minute here. Early this morning, I received a weird phone call at work, and some idiot started coughing in the phone.

Was that you Carmelo? His blank stare explodes into laugher, and almost choked while taking a sip. "Well, I'm glad that you're amused, because that was one of the reasons that I had a bad day. Curiosity was killing me, I even dialed back the number, but couldn't get through. You came to mind, but I seriously doubted that it was you." "Hey, what was I supposed to do, come up there and wait for you in the parking lot, and humiliate myself as you drive away with your new boyfriend?" "Well that would have been nice; don't you think that I'm worth a little fist fight, afraid to get your little nails broken pretty boy?" "Well I had to be creative, and trust me, it was much better than Sean's plan, who wanted to be Mr. Magnum P.I on a late night stakeout."

"Well you surely made up for it, and you're fortunate that things worked out for you. Carmelo I'm single. I've been single for almost a year now. I tried to reach out to you on Thanks Giving, but you never returned my call." "I was pissed, mommy gave me the message but I had some issues to work out. My heart was broken, and you had made it clear that you had moved on." "That guy was such an idiot, I'm soo happy that I didn't sleep with him." It certainly wasn't Carmelo's concern, and was over that being a possibility by this point. She continued to vent as her bills became too excessive, and moved into an apartment that was in Springfield. A few days prior, she decided to accept a full time position at the detention center. She kept herself busy with work, as her son Dane moved to Florida to be with his father. All good news for Carmelo, who is beside himself with excitement, as her tone speaks volumes of sexual frustration. Another glass of wine with beef sliders and a salad for both is ordered, while he practices his listening skills. His eye contact expresses deep concern, and his posture attentive. "This year has been one hell of a roller coaster ride for me. But I'm glad that I've got my health. I'm sorry for ranting. Enough about me how are you doing?" Before answering, he calls Stanford to check in, and is told by the old man to take his time and don't let that pretty little thing get away, or he'll order a ship load of Viagra.

He obeys, then answers, he also has moved, and is working two jobs, but will be returning to school shortly to finish up undergrad. By now, I think you would agree that Carmelo loves money and his lifestyle that's fulfilled with dining at the best restaurants in the city. So he doesn't over react when Adriane expresses her disappointment about his hiatus from school. While cracking a smile, he reminds her of the additional money that would be saved by having some of their late night rondevu's at his place. "It's around the corner from mommy, she wouldn't let me go too far." With almost an hour remaining, hey pays the check and they go for a quick stroll near, Table 31. The steakhouse bistro was one of the very few elegant places that Carmelo has not experienced with their beautiful fountain display that lined the outside seating area. The newly planted trees were decorated with white Christmas lights, as they held hands while strolling down the designer pavement. It's been exactly two and a half hours and they begin heading back. Upon arrival, they both enter the building, with nature calling. As she walks by, Carmelo catches Stanford glancing at her physique, but remains silent and allows the old man to enjoy himself. We're all happy for Carmelo. He had blossomed into a mature young man and established a healthy relationship. Adriane had become like the universe to him. Every day for the next several months was like a new source of joy.

He decides to be a little spontaneous and fulfill his boredom, and invite Adriane to his job in Manayunk. He manipulated the five foot, Hispanic maintenance guy by establishing trust and expressing a general concern for the tenants and possible guest. "Donny, there's some tenants and guest coming in pretty late and using the staff bathroom, I don't want to inconvenience anyone by having them wait, so can you leave the model home open so that I can utilize the facilities when needed ?" "I won't leave it open, but I'll give you the key, just be sure to lock the door when your finish." Carmelo couldn't help laughing! A group of intoxicated girls are heading out but stops by the front desk and begin flirting with him but he politely dismisses them seconds before Adriane arrives. She follows his directions of simply getting out and proceed through the first numbered red door. Its midnight and the building is dead. Perfect timing for his shenanigans! He flipped around the desk sign mentioning that he was making rounds and head over to meet Adriane. When opening the door of the gorgeously decorated modeled townhouse, she awaited him in the master bedroom laced with burgundy Victoria secret lingerie. Their careful, not to ruin the sheets and Carmelo enjoys his forty five minute bathroom break. Ha Ha Ha!

A few weeks later, his boss Marissa is promoted and transferred to another location in the city. A new manager arrives and Carmelo immediately catches a bad vibe. Mandy Brenner was a fair looking brunette. Her unprofessionalism by not introducing herself, and just simply providing Carmelo with his paycheck on that Happy Friday, was laughable. He simply preferred the old fashion way instead of direct deposit, while avoiding the swindling bank fees. A month later Ms. Brenner left a voice message, informing him not to clock in on his next scheduled day, and to go straight to her office. Of course the property had surveillance and he suspected that his amorous events with Adriane had been exposed. To his surprise, here's the filth that this power crazy woman brought to his attention. "Thank you for coming in Carmelo, I received a complaint yesterday that you have been looking at some of the women in the building and the records were checked which you failed to log the delivery of flowers for a tenant, which are both violations of company policy."

Sitting there peering at her, his first initial response was going to be "First and foremost racist, this is 2010, not 1810, and we're in the north. I understand your eagerness to carry on tradition, but I'm free to look at whoever I please. I'm basically a glorified security guard, and it's my job to observe the premises." All true, but with that response, he would have gotten himself fired by the martinet. But instead, Carmelo implements the fundamentals and lesson number one of *48 Laws of power,* from bestselling authors, Robert Greene and Joost Elffers. "Always make those above you feel comfortably superior. In your desire to please or impress them, do not go too far in displaying your talents or you might accomplish the opposite – inspire fear and insecurity. Make your masters appear more brilliant than they are and you will attain the heights of power." Carmelo managed to escape with just one lash of a written warning, but a month later, Mandy rewarded him with a full time position that included pretty good benefits. He reconstructed his schedule so that there's no conflict and the four to twelve shift is quite gratifying. His center city job is reserved for the weekends and he's now working sixty hours each week. It was unclear whether this woman was attracted to him, and unaware of how to express herself or suffered from bipolar disorder. Facts regarding Mandy's emotions were confirmed as her pregnancy became noticeable along with a massive amount of weight gain. Carmelo decided to extend his appreciation and one evening as Mandy prepared to leave, but remained a complete grouch, he surprised her with a set of extremely soft pillows from Home Goods, a few Bath and Bodyworks products, and a gift card from Old Navy. Excellent timing as she was given a surprised baby shower the next day by the executives. He was able to see the bigger picture and that included his future with Adriane. She was also very persuasive in having him get rid of his shoe box and start acting like an adult. "If someone steals your shoe box, you'll be left with nothing, but if the bank is robbed you'll be reimbursed any lost wages. That's a pretty good reason to charge someone a small fee to protect their money." His account was significant due to minimizing his spending and it was officially time to create new memories.

# Chapter 18
# It's Official

*High Times*

Still playing with fire by having entertainment while supposed to be working. He informs Stanford of his plan to invite Adriane down for a visit. "No problem young Johnson, I see that you're keeping a pretty good grip on this one." "Yup! But I've decided to make it a little bit tighter. She's worth it, and I'm almost up there with you old timer." "Carmelo you're only twenty seven are you sure?" "My Grandpa Glenn always says, people can never be too sure in this kind of situation but every man must know his limits. I'll be twenty eight soon and lost track of how many women I've been with. I never encountered any life threatening diseases, but I've lost numerous friends to the streets before their twenty fifth birthday and it's clear that I'm here for a reason and some adjustments have to be made so I can continue to strive for greatness." "Well said, then go for it. What do you have in mind?" "Let's just say that we'll be above the city tonight." After making his rounds, and realizing that all of the staff and executives were gone, he sends a text and Adriane replies that she'll be there around eight o'clock. He strongly suggest eleven, so she doesn't have to sit and wait for him. But she objects due to having to work in the morning. He assures her that it will be worth the hassle and she arrives right on time looking irritable. Stanford is thrilled and grinning wildly, exposing all rotten dentures.

Carmelo punches the clock and takes her by the hand, escorting her to the elevator. "Where are we going" "Relax, I want to show you something." His ears are clogged but are cleared once they hit the twenty ninth floor. There's another flight of stairs that leads to the roof, but before taking the next step, she gives him a dirty look. "Why are we going to the roof, are you trying to get rid of me?" "No silly, come on, we're almost there" and playfully adds "You could also use the exercise." They made their way up the steps and both were out of breath. He opens the door and the view of our beloved city of Philadelphia is astounding. There's a slight breeze dancing with Adriane's hair, as she remains speechless. The statue of William Penn appears to be gazing at them, while observing the stunning beauty of the Betsy Ross Bridge. "Unbelievable, isn't it" he whispers, "It's ok", with a sexy smirk while placing her arms around his neck. Seconds later, I, Sean and Eden appear with Carmelo's parents, which obviously frightens her.

Carmelo was even a bit startled and he was the mastermind. Samantha and Rachel, her classmates from nursing school appeared holding each other with tears gushing. Jared and Yvette were able to make the trip from their home in Illinois to be a part of this chapter leading up to the big day. Carmelo has been planning this since his evening with Adriane at the Four Seasons hotel. His legs trembled when attempting to bend them, and stared into her eyes to gather himself. He took a deep breath before going down on both knees, revealed the high quality stone tucked away in his red pocket square, and begged for her to be his wife. They were married late august of 2010 at the Springfield Country Club, with all parties in attendants and a selective guest list. They officially moved in their new apartment for Christmas. Despite drinking socially, Adriane overall maintained a great standard of health and watched her blood pressure.

There was no need for in vitro fertilization, just a little extra love and they celebrated the New Year, expecting twins. Alana and Connor were born five pounds three ounces and completely healthy. Within two years, Carmelo and Adriane began a lucrative day care center in Springfield. Last summer 2013, they purchased a Villa in Jamaica and invited my entire family on vacation. Now that he has officially become part of the bondage club, Carmelo actually feels like a ton of bricks have been removed off his shoulders, and welcomes the new obstacles of marriage. "It's a fresh start in experiencing truly being in love with a woman, without pretending, so that I can continue to receive the huge benefits of convenience. I can enjoy my children without the unnecessary drama. I'm probably spending more money now than ever before, but it's worth every penny to ensure my family's lifestyle, now that my pursuit of happiness has concluded."

*The Beginning*
*By,*
*Cornell Richards*

## Thank You's and Dedication

To The Firm, I'm wishing you guys the greatest blessings one can endure, Branden, Kev, Darnell, and Manhee peace and love. I would like to wish all my former colleagues the best from the Cardinal Krol Center, Ali, Emperor (Omar), Sonny, Sam Binda, David Rowe, Geba, Kia, Teta, Esther, Julius, Tashi Rowe, April Jordan, Jennifer Brown you make beautiful babies., Maureen, Melvin, Aaron, Phil, AL, Adam, Big Steve, Big Rowlin, Emecca, John, Kevilyn Boyle, Anthony, Nicole, Mgr. Kelly, Serita, and Ruth Hill, and Andrea Joseph.

Thank you to my Venice Lofts tenants and former Colleagues for your encouragement and feedback. Mr. Phil, Kim Hall, Al Moore, Stacey Muse, Neil Hollander, Eric Narodovich Greg Marsala, Dr. Roth, Barrie Fisher, Melonease Shaw, Jaime Cantanese , Maurice Hawkins and family, Shareem and Latisha Hargrove, Christine and Josh Marks, Peter Lyons, Naimah Moore, Mahari Bailey and his beautiful family, Danielle and Johnathan Parsell. April Eggleston, your truly blessed, please display your experiences that will surely enspire others. Angle Cherry, you were surely an experience. Ha Ha !Thank you Mrs. Lavaina Muse for being the first to confirm on keeping this project clean and not typical, and Lindsay Hurst, thanks for letting me borrow your place, I had a ball. Ha Ha! To. Tieasha Miller, thank you for being the first to suggest that this should be an independent project and my apologies for being stubborn.

To my grandparents George and Joan Gray who have recently celebrated their eighty-first birthday, please keep making the carrot juice. My brother Shawn and Uncle Pete, stay strong, everyday above ground is a blessing. To my cousin Renee, Jackie, Munchie thank you for your services in the Army. Aunt Valurie and Cousin Karen and Iley. To my aunts and uncle along with host of cousins in Canada. My Dewey Street family, Ant, Mrs. Margerate, Kia, Mr. Ike (R.I.P), E, Sabron (Great Sermon), Makia, Lynette, Charelle, Ms. Connie, Lamar, Row, Uncle Greg, Damien and Candace Jones, James, Insunn, Kev (NJ) , Byron, (Ms. Betty R.I.P) PJ, Darnell, Dina, Dora, Ms. Mary, Twink, Carla, Sam, Akeem, Blade, Jay, Alicia, Jackie, Ms. Carlene, Ms. Phyllis, We're all still here and doing well. To my sixty first street family, Steve, Malcom, and the whole entire Rice family, Mally, Ms. Shabby, Wakeem, Shakida, Tiffany, Tasha, Ebony, Reece, Laurie, Jalil, Shannon, Troy, Montey and her grandmother, Jeff, David, Kev, Darnell, Daniel, Rapheal, stay strong and keep your head up. To my Edgewood street family, Markes, Michelle, Saheed, Slim, Huck, Greg, (Sadot R.I.P) Ant, Jarves, Ivin, Rog, Sean, and Lamar. Old friends from Sayre Middle School and Vine street, Kenny Jackson, Buhdah, (Fat Boy R.I.P) John Smith, Kaheem Weatherspoon, Kahlil Johnson. To my Robinson Str. family, Tone and Deacon Jim, Mike and his beautiful sisters I'm single, Duck, Steve, Big Chris, Bossy, Jimmy, Rasheeda, Brooke, Chris (country) Raheem . To everyone on Millick street, Mike, Courtney, Mal Mal, Sharon, Kamal, Shy, Tone and Chris Wallace. To my Sixty second/ Felton str. Family Mal, Sparkle, Passion Vincent, keep making great music I'll trade you a book for a CD, (R.I.P Joey), Brandon, Lil Will, Donte, Chop and Dog, Naheem, Rell, Derrick, and Marlon, Big Tez. To my 58th street family, Wayne, (Ra Ra R.I.P) Nard, Diddy, Omar, Daron, Derek, (Dev R.I.P), Chauncey, Snuff, Wesley, keep your head up. Champ, keep your head up, Mikey F (R.I.P). Ms. Lucy and Danny, I apologize for my distance, I will be visiting you shortly. Old friends from John Barry Elementary School and my first and basketball coach Mr. Johnson and Mr. Keys, Elijah aka Black and his beautiful sisters, Brian, Mike Carroll, Poppa Do, Tyreke, Warren, Norman, James Struggs. My Sayre middle basketball coach Mr. Sherlds, my Rosery crew, Isaiah Ham, Sean G, Cerel, Matt, Cherelle, Haneef, Reg, Sean, Lindsay. Ms. Wanda, Ms. Trina, Dewey, Malikah thanks for all the kisses, The twins, Drew and Anwar, You guys are grown now and have no clue who I am. Nakisha Jones stay beautiful. My Overbrook family, Kenny, Anthony, Mr. &Ms. Bowler, Vanisha, Will. To everyone on 66$^{th}$ street Ms. Karen, Alvin, Ella her brother Anthony and family, Kisha, great job with the kids. Ms. Peggy, Mr. Chris, Mr. Kev Lawanda Mason, Jay, Chuck, Amber, Eric, Ms. B and family, and Cordell.

Thank you Mrs. Dahpne Daniels you've been a wonderful God Mother for Trish. Virginia Vassell, Cousin Lydia, Aunt Beryl, Nate Da Great, Sister Morgan thank you for all the prayers. My Aunt Dottie, back home in Jamaica, stay strong until I pay you a visit.

Kind regards and a **Special thanks,** to Eric Bonaparte, Fredrick Perry, and Sean Andrews. These Kings kept me under there shield during my unexpected vacation.

**This book is dedicated to my great friends Juilan "Juice" Madison, John "Jizz" Custus, and Sean "Shiz" May, who unfortunately passed away, but ignited my passion to continue with this epic tale.**

**Rest peacefully in the house of Glory.**